THE WITCHES OF SCOTLAND

THE DREAM DANCERS: AKASHIC CHRONICLES - BOOK 1

STEVEN P AITCHISON

CYT MEDIA LTD

This novel's story and characters are fictitious. Certain long-standing institutions, agencies, and public offices are mentioned, as are street names, but the characters involved are wholly imaginary.

Steven Aitchison

The Akashic Chronicles

The Witches of Scotland Series: Glasgow

ISBN: 978-1838032777

© 2022, Steven Aitchison / CYT Media LTD

FOLLOW AND LIKE

Steven's TikTok Page

www.TikTok.com/@steven_p_aitchison

Email

authorsteven@stevenaitchison.co.uk

I respond to all emails personally, so drop me a note or a question, and I will be more than happy to answer you. I honestly love talking with my readers, so I don't think I am different from you because I have published a book. Drop me a note to say hello.

BECOME A MEMBER OF THE WITCHES OF SCOTLAND COMMUNITY BY JOINING MY NEWSLETTER. CLICK THE LINK BELOW.

https://www.stevenaitchison.co.uk/wos

When you join the newsletter, I will send out updates about the Witches of Scotland series and give free character bios, and images.

You'll also get free excerpts of upcoming books as well as short stories, and video updates from me too.

You can become a beta reader for future books and be part of this journey with me.

PROLOGUE

$\mathcal{B}$udapest, six months ago

The medical lab was small when compared to the other ViraTech labs around the world, and only three scientists had worked there for the last eighteen months.

For good reason.

The virus had taken fourteen months to perfect, and it was time to test it on the world.

The ten armed guards walked the perimeter of the facility in turns. It took sixteen minutes to complete a full circuit. When not walking the perimeter, each guard trekked slowly from building to fence, sweeping their eyes from left to right. The security system was so sensitive if a rabbit happened to hop past the area, it would trigger the lights and ten MP5k machine guns.

Jessica Campbell floated inside the facility, watching the lab workers gingerly move about the room. Their arm-length rubber gloves and gas masks hinted at the volatility of what they held. She observed them from the corner of the ceiling since the view was far more advantageous.

This is it. Be calm. You've got five minutes to get this right.

She had to keep her heart rate slow and steady or risk being catapulted back to Edinburgh in milliseconds.

The lab workers, two men and one woman, didn't speak to each other tonight. Normally, they were a chatty bunch as they worked, having grown close over the last year and a half. They often talked about the money they would receive after successfully completing this assignment. Everyone had agreed to quit their jobs as epidemiologists and travel abroad.

Tonight, they were close to the payoff, close to ending the sleepless nights, the worry, the guilt. They all knew, of course, that the payoff wouldn't really have that effect. The results of all their hard work would only add to their anxiety. The deaths of millions of older people around the world would forever be on their consciences, and Jessie knew they had all asked them-selves if it would be worth it. Would never worrying about money be enough to assuage their guilt?

That's when rationalisation and justification entered the equation. How did you press forward, otherwise? She had often heard their weak justifications as they worked. They told themselves older adults were a drain on the economy, a drain on pensions, on healthcare services, on the welfare state and employment figures.

Not to mention a drain on families.

They had a job to do tonight, and they did it in silence.

Jessica knew the time had finally come to materialise and stop the virus from being unleashed. She also knew the consequences if she failed and fought hard to control her racing pulse. Her vision faded in and out as her energy levels spiked.

Come on! You've got this...calm...deep breaths...in through your nose, out through your mouth.

She breathed a sigh of relief as her vision remained fixed, her heart rate slow and steady. She lowered herself down to ground level, preparing to materialise.

One of the lab workers turned around suddenly and looked straight at her. He couldn't see her, but she knew he must have sensed something or felt her energy. He continued to look at her and around her. Jessica stayed still, willing him to get back to work. He glanced at the others and then back at Jessica. After seeing no reaction from his co-workers, he shook it off and continued. The scientists packed a sturdy casing with ten large glass vials.

Jessica considered all the months of planning involved to prepare for this moment. She was instrumental in this mission's success or failure. Her training had been intense and stressful, made even more so due to their timeline and what was at stake, not to mention the negative impact heavy practice had on her body. There were only so many times a person could travel before it took its toll on both body and mind.

She crouched low, waiting for her moment, thinking about the day her father had first revealed the threat of the virus not four months ago. Dream dancers were diligent in their quest to elevate humanity, and any threats to that were promptly reported and addressed. One particular dream dancer had been "astral sniffing" when he stumbled upon the threat, immediately reporting it to her father. The head of this organisation was an unknown, but the labs were easily located.

Outraged, her father had recruited her and another dream dancer to spy on the facility, but they had not been prepared for the virus to be ready so soon. No other dream dancers had been trained to "port," over vast distances such as Edinburgh to Boston. So, her training had been intense. She just hoped she could pull it off now.

Jessica took a deep breath and slowly crept up behind the three scientists as they put the remaining vials into the foam-moulded casing. Once the last vial was secured, they closed it.

This is it.

Jessica's pulse rose again in anticipation, her vision

becoming a little blurry as she looked from worker to worker. She had to act now before they padlocked it.

She closed her eyes and visualised the light and energy rising from the soles of her feet up to the crown of her head and beyond. Sensation soon followed. She'd practised this hundreds of times before, so it was relatively easy, but there was still a part of her that wondered if it would work in this type of setting.

When it really mattered.

When it would save millions of lives.

Only thirty seconds to do it.

Her body materialised in front of the lab workers. At first, they couldn't quite comprehend what was happening, which bought Jessica a little more time.

Shit, I'm losing it.

She wasn't materialising quickly enough, not as she had in training. One scientist stood back, his mouth agape.

Shit, he's going to scream.

Much to her relief, her materialisation sped up. Although it took only a few seconds, it felt like an age.

With the lab workers temporarily stunned, Jessica grabbed the case of ten vials and tipped it onto the ground, smashing the glass and releasing a noxious gas capable of killing them all within twenty seconds of inhalation.

Jessie noted one vial had remained intact.

Seventeen seconds to go.

She took the empty case and smashed it down on the unbroken vial.

Fourteen seconds to go.

She would be dead, too, if she didn't hurry this up. The vapours of gas from the vials began to rise and hiss, spreading over the floor of the lab.

The scientists stood motionless for a few seconds, confusion and disbelief paralysing their movements. And then they ran for the exit.

Jessica, despite being at the back, ported to the exit before them and pressed the emergency shut-in button. This would lock and seal the room in case of extreme emergency.

Nine seconds to go.

The fumes from the vials filled the room. The scientists still had their masks on, remaining safe but still confused as they tried to keep track of Jessica.

She appeared and disappeared as if blinking in and out of existence, unlocking each of their masks and ripping them off. It was done so quickly; they didn't have time to react and immediately started coughing and spluttering.

Jessica quickly crossed the room to the sealed cabinet and reached her hand in to unlock the door.

She located the laptops and notebooks needing to be destroyed as they contained all the formulas, notes, videos and everything else required to make the deadly virus. She flipped the laptops revealing the base.

Five seconds to go, and I'll be dead, too.

The bottles of fluoroantimonic acid had been placed in the cabinet's bottom a few days ago, carefully hidden behind a pile of notepads.

Jessica grabbed the steel bottle holder and quickly poured the acid crystals over the notebooks and bottoms of the laptops. The sulfuric acid was then poured over the crystals, which immediately started fuming and burning through the paper and laptops. The acid corroded the tech and paper, destroying the white tiles beneath.

She had to get out of there in case the acids reacted with the oxygen in the air, and there were only a few seconds left.

She quickly scanned the room, noting the dead workers.

Two seconds to go.

Closing her eyes, she visualised her next destination, the security room, but lost her focus. She opened her eyes in alarm, noting she was still in the lab. The fumes were about to engulf her, too.

The masks! Where did I leave the masks?

Jessica coughed as she kept low and to the edges of the room. She felt her way toward the main door where the scientists had collapsed.

Why the hell didn't I grab a mask?

Finding one on the ground, she quickly pulled it on, worried she hadn't made it in time. She was now surrounded by white smoke.

She closed her eyes again and visualised the security room.

Her port was violent due to the adrenaline that was coursing round her body, and she nearly landed on top of the guard who was staring at the security screen in horror at the dead scientists. His shock made him slow to react.

Before his hand hit the alarm, Jessica snapped it, shattering his radius and ulna bones at the same time. The guard let out an almighty scream and clutched his arm. She grabbed the back of his head and slammed it against his workstation, knocking him out instantly.

After flinging off her mask, she quickly tapped on the keys and found the recording for that day. She located the footage of herself entering the room. It looked like static as she flitted in and out of the picture. With the speed and agility of a hacker, Jessica deleted the recording from the records and backup drive.

She didn't kill the guard, feeling certain his story of events would be just too unbelievable. The scientists had died within seconds of being exposed to the virus. That would be the story, and she didn't feel bad for them. They had known the evil of their creation and its consequences.

Money. It was always about money.

Jessica closed her eyes and pictured herself outside the medical facility. She projected and then studied the guards surrounding the area. They seemed none the wiser, still completing their clockwork rounds.

It would take at least ten hours before anybody knew what had happened inside the medical lab. It would never be reported in the news, but there would be a backlash.

She closed her eyes again and was transported back to Edinburgh where her body lay in a secure room.

Jessica opened her eyes and sought her father out through the viewing window.

Her father, eyes wide, searched her expression for confirmation. Jessica nodded and gave him an encouraging smile. The mission had been a success.

The relief on his face was shared by other dream dancers present. He released a deep breath, as if he had been holding it in for hours. Jessica sat up, coughing uncontrollably. She took a glass of water from the side cabinet next to her bed as the group from the program gathered together at the window, all seven of them, including her father.

She raised her thumbs in the air and smiled while everyone cheered and celebrated.

Yet Jessica Campbell knew this wasn't over. Not by a long shot. And she couldn't do it alone. Her father, Dr. Joseph Campbell, and the team from the Koestler Institute were adamant about finding more dream dancers to assist them in their fight, keeping tabs on the energetic fields of many potentials from around the world.

Jessica had been following the astral movements of one very promising dream dancer from her home country of Scotland.

It was time to pay a visit to David Hunter.

CHAPTER 1

*A*s he sat outside the student advisors' offices, David Hunter's thoughts turned to his dreams. His obsession with the dream world was the very reason he sat in that hard, cold chair, trying to save his academic career. He had been practising lucid dreaming for years now, ever since his parents had abandoned him as a young child.

Lucid dreaming had become his escape from a world he didn't particularly like or feel he belonged in.

Unfortunately, he owed his aunt for taking him in, and studying law was his way of thanking Aunt Gen for not dumping him with social services and letting them foster him out. Since there was a whole line of Hunters who had become successful lawyers in the past, his career path seemed obvious.

He didn't like it. Bored him to tears, really, but there

wasn't a career out there that utilised a skill like lucid dreaming, so law it had to be.

"David Hunter?" said the stern looking secretary.

"Yes. Yes, that's me," he said, standing and walking toward the woman with a clipboard nestled in her arm. She looked over her horn-rimmed glasses at him.

"This way, David."

The female advisor behind the desk briefly glanced at David as he entered the room, motioning for him to sit in the chair in front of her. She continued to write as the phone rang. Pressing a button, she cut off the shrill tone and turned the full force of her attention on him.

David flashed a smile, maintaining eye contact. Charm had gotten him this far in life, and he would use it to get him out of this mess. Fortunately, she was an attractive thirty-something brunette, with dark olive skin, very little makeup, and dressed in nice business attire. The plaque on her desk read Amisha Bhatia.

Amisha rolled her eyes, which took David by surprise.

"You're in deep shit here, Mr. Hunter, so drop the pretty boy, flirting routine."

"Well, that's not very cordial now is it..." he looked at her name plate again "Amisha." He was a little taken aback but liked her fire.

"Yeah, well, we've no time for pleasantries. That seems to have been your problem all along."

"And where is Danielle?" David asked, referring to

his previous advisor, one who had been much more appreciative of his pretty boy, flirting routine.

"I've taken your case over from Danielle, as this has escalated to the progress committee, and you're in danger of being thrown out of the university."

"I'm sure we can work something out," David said as he picked up a paperweight from her desk. The look on her face told him she didn't like that move.

"Do you think your aunt's money and influence is going to carry you through the last two years of your degree? No! You actually have to put in the work and pass the exams. No passing of exams means no little piece of paper to say you graduated and no little job in a solicitors' office being the tea boy for a few years."

She stood up and took a thick folder from the book-shelves behind her.

She dropped it with a thump on the desk. "This is a list of all the people who have been thrown out of university. Every single one of them were given multiple chances to buck up, but they were still thrown out. Their money, their family name, and their status weren't enough to buy them their degree, and you sure as hell will not buy your way through it, either, unless you're just sickeningly wealthy."

David put his hand in his pocket and pulled out some loose change. "Well, I do have exactly three pounds and twenty-eight pence, but..." He held up his forefinger as if just remembering something. "I get my student loan payment at the end of the week, so maybe we could," he held up two hands and see-sawed them, "you know, come to some sort of arrangement."

She laughed derisively and shook her head. "You don't have the money, but your Aunty Genevieve Hunter does. If it wasn't for her, you would have been thrown out a long time ago."

David sighed in mock defeat. "What the hell is it with all the hostility? I'm here to get advice and representation from you."

"No! You're here to study. You're here to get a law degree with hard work and effort. What you are not here to do is go out on the piss and get stoned with your friends every night. I've got another meeting with the progress committee in a few weeks, and if I don't get reports of improvement, I will have to recommend that *their* recommendation of dismissal be upheld. You've got exactly two weeks to resubmit two, fifteen-hundred-word essays and resit the two exams you failed."

"Okey dokey, I think I can manage that."

The student advisor stared at him, appearing weary. "What do you want to do with your life, David? What is your purpose?"

"My purpose? I'm twenty-two years old. I don't have a purpose." David ran his hands through his unkempt hair.

Amisha walked over to the window and looked out onto University Avenue. He did his best to avoid gazing at her rear.

"We all have a purpose, David. I suggest you go

away and think about yours as I don't see it being at Glasgow University." She turned and gave him one last reproachful stare before waving him out of her office.

David rose from his seat and walked out of the room smiling.

He kept that smile firmly affixed until the advisors' offices were far behind him.

Shit!

David walked slowly down the steps of the student services building, trying to figure out what he would say to Aunt Gen.

Shit! Shit! Shit!

Making his way down University Avenue, David considered the consequences he faced if thrown out of university.

Why the hell didn't I do something about this before?

He knew the answer already. His Aunt Gen always bailed him out. Her loyalty to his parents was something he'd taken full advantage of over the years. She wasn't going to be happy about this at all, and she wouldn't be able to bail him out of this one.

He thought about her disappointment in him. She might not say anything, but her silence was often worse than her censure.

With his head down, he walked past the Bower Building and on to the medical school. The light from the sun bounced off the car windows as he took off his jacket and slung it over his shoulder. The West End of Glasgow was always thriving, always so full of energy. It was a unique atmosphere from anywhere else in the city.

David could never figure out why it felt that way to him, but he supposed it was the mix of affluence and intelligence. After all, Glasgow University was at the heart of it all, and the property prices were exorbitant, meaning only the wealthy could afford to live here and rent out property to the students.

He loved it but knew it was his aunt who had made living here and attending university possible. Without her, he would never have been able to stay in this part of the city.

As he walked, he thought back to the conversation with the student advisor. Then thoughts of his absent parents made an appearance. He got angry as that old, familiar "Fuck you, world!" attitude built within him.

Trying to distract himself, he thought about his most recent adventures in the lucid dream world. A place where he belonged. A place of his own creation. An amazing world where he could meet different people, have sex with beautiful women, literally fly around the world, soar around the cosmos, and speak to his dead grandparents. The lucid dream world was his escape, his passion, his solace, his place to hide from the realities of his existence.

And yet, he had no idea how he did it. The question remained after years of lucid dreaming. How was it possible that he, of all people, could do it?

Was it just an escape from the reality of life or was

life an escape from the reality of his dreams? His fascination had deepened over the years, and his studies had led him to some amazing people in the field, not to mention some weird and wonderful Reddit boards.

Focus!

What would he tell Aunt Gen and his friends?

Christ, what will I do for a job?

That thought scared him more than the thought of any arguments he might have with his aunt.

He didn't have any skills or experience in anything other than studying...or pretending to study. He felt a weight pressing on his chest, and his breathing became laboured as he realised the gravity of his situation.

Shit! What the hell am I going to do?

Cars, vans, buses and motorcycles queued on Byres Road. The noise of the traffic, the low hum of people talking around him, and the general business amped up his anxiety concerning his pending confrontation with Aunt Gen.

He slipped between the traffic and crossed to Dowanside Road, walking quickly with his shoulders hunched.

He stared at his front door for a good ten minutes before mustering up the courage to enter. As he twisted the yale lock and gently pushed the door open, he heard his Aunt Gen speaking on the phone and pulled back slightly.

"...he's not exhibited any signs after all this time, so I think it's safe to say he's not going to." She stopped to listen. "Oh yes, it's a blessing as he'll be out of any danger. I don't know if I would want this world given the choice." She laughed and paused again to listen.

David's toe caught on the rug, causing him to stumble.

She turned around, startled. "David!" Putting her lips closer to the mouthpiece she whispered, "I'll call you back later."

David closed the door and took off his jacket.

"I think it's time we had a talk, don't you?"

With his back turned to her, David grimaced and rolled his eyes.

Here it comes. That didn't take long at all.

He drew in a deep breath and turned to face his Aunt Gen.

She might have been small, but her words always packed a punch, and from the look on her face, censure rather than silence was forthcoming. This was going to be a beating.

"How are you?" David said, lifting his voice, trying to sound cheerful and nonchalant.

"Don't you give me that. I got a call from Danielle. What's going on at university?" She placed her hands on her hips which was always frightening.

"Aunt Gen, it's not a good time for lectures."

"It never is, David," she said, looking at him with narrowed eyes. "You're failing all your exams, you're out drinking with your friends most nights, and you bring home girls I don't even know. I give you as much leeway as possible, David, but you're throwing it all back in my face." Her voice became higher pitched the longer she spoke. She disliked giving lectures just as much as David disliked hearing them.

"If you get thrown out of university, you'll have to move out. As much as I hate doing it, you need a bit of tough love."

"Yeah, coz I've never really had any other kind of love, right?" David said, referring to his parents.

"Oh, for goodness' sake, we've been over this. I know this haunts you, child, but you have to believe me when I say your parents didn't abandon you."

"Aunt Gen, I'm not a child, but you keep treating me like one. You keep telling me they didn't abandon me, but you have no other explanation to offer. They dropped me off at your doorstep and disappeared. From where I'm standing, that's abandonment. I haven't seen them for eighteen years. I don't know if they're dead or alive, so tell me something, anything, for Christ's sake."

"Be very careful of the way you speak to me, David."

"Not going to address it, then? I'm twenty-two years old and have nothing. And where am I going to go if you throw me out?" David ran his hands through his hair and then rubbed his face. It had been a shit day, and this had made it worse.

"I warned you months ago that the deal was you could stay here rent free as long as you did well at university." Aunt Gen turned away, pacing in front of the bay windows as David sat on the brown Chester-field sofa opposite.

"I mean, what is it you want to do? What is your purpose in life, David?"

He looked at her askance, brows furrowed. That was the second time he'd been asked that question today.

He shook his head and raised his hands in defeat. "I don't know." His throat was tight with emotion, and he could feel the tears pressing the backs of his eyes. He swallowed hard and kept his mouth closed, blinking quickly to stop the tears from rolling.

"Well, you better decide quickly, or you'll be out on your ear with no prospects, no job, and no experience. No doubt you'll get some girl pregnant, then you'll be living on benefits in a council house somewhere, scraping by to make ends meet every week." Her voice became even more shrill.

"What would you know about benefits and living in council houses?" he shouted, his anger exploding.

His aunt's face darkened with colour. "I fuckin' lived that life when I was younger. I stayed in a crappy council tenement, married to a loser with two kids to raise on my own. I took you in and loved you as my own. I fuckin' know that life all too well, and I'm trying to keep you from going down that road, you selfish little shit." Tears sprang to Aunt Gen's eyes as she turned and looked out the window. "And I can't...I can't tell you anything about your mother and father. It's for your own good. Don't you see that?"

David shot to his feet, anger and hurt burning within him. "No, I don't see that. I don't see it at all. I was four years old when they left me here, and you haven't told me why. I don't know if they're dead or alive, but most of the time I wish they were dead. Better that than living in this world with no desire to see me." He hurried out of the drawing room and ran upstairs to his bedroom.

He slammed the door and threw himself onto his bed, staring daggers at the ceiling. He'd really done it this time. Aunt Gen never swore. His angry thoughts thrashed about, fighting to make sense of things. All he got for those efforts was the beginning of a migraine.

Exhaustion tugged at the corners of his mind, and he gratefully allowed it to take him, knowing he'd find relief on the other side.

CHAPTER 2

*I*t was the usual drift into the lucid realm with David asking himself constantly, "Am I dreaming?" He tested the hypothesis that he was dreaming every time he did this, usually by trying to read the nearest book, newspaper, or a window sign. This time, he decided to float aimlessly until he stumbled upon something of interest.

He hovered in the middle of Sauchiehall Street for a second as shoppers passed him, some looking at him strangely. He didn't care, this was his dream. He started to spin on the spot and soon catapulted into the air, flying around Glasgow city centre.

That elation of becoming conscious in his dream never left him. The exhilaration, the excitement, that feeling of being in control and having power over the direction of his own life was beyond amazing. He had left the real world behind; this was *his* world.

He watched the people below as they pointed at him while he navigated his way across the skies of Glasgow. Even now, all of this was his own making. He'd created all the people down below, the buildings, the cars, the buses, the birds, everything. It was his imagination in action, and he marvelled at it as the rush of air flowed over him.

Banking left, he dove toward The Royal Concert Hall and landed on the roof. He squatted low and studied the people walking up Buchanan Street. There were thousands of them just like there were on a busy weekend.

This is all my creation.

He zeroed in on the faces of some of the shoppers: men and women of all ages, young children, and even animals.

Why? Why are all these people in my dream? Why did I create them?

Just then, a creature appeared beside him, as so often happened. He wasn't sure why his mind had seen fit to drum up the strange beast, but he'd gotten used to it. He'd even started having conversations with it. After all, the gargoyle was his creation.

Yet this time was a little different.

"Things are changing, David." The creature said it with a hint of sadness in his voice. David looked at him, eyes narrowed, and forehead creased. The creature had never addressed him by name. "The energy of the world is being depleted, and it will have an effect on human evolution."

"What does that mean? I don't understand." David wanted to see where this conversation would go. Maybe he could give himself the answers to his own predicament. After all, it was his mind he spoke to.

The golden-coloured body of the creature shimmered.

That's new.

Its tiny skeletal wings flapped slowly, preparing itself for flight. The two horns atop its head glowed as well.

What's going on here?

"As I said, things are changing. You're going to have to make a decision soon, and it's not going to be an easy one to make." The tiny tail of the creature began to move back and forth, and the horns lining its small spine rippled with light.

"Listen, I really don't understand what you're talking about...what I'm talking about. It's been a weird couple of days, and it's obviously spilling over into my dreams..."

The creature interrupted him. "You think this isn't real? Just a figment of your imagination? This is not a dream, David. I am not your creation. This is the stepping-stone to another world. A bridge between the earth plane and the astral plane. This is partly your mind and partly a window to the astral planes."

"Astral planes?" David said slowly. "We've had multiple conversations, and you've never once brought this up."

He'd heard of the astral realm but had never heard it referred to in the plural. It made him nervous.

If I haven't heard that before, then surely...I can't know what I don't know!

"How many astral planes are there?" he asked, looking down at the creature who now stood as high as his shoulder.

"Seven. Well, ten in total, but seven main planes of existence, and a few of them are divided into two."

Interesting. And absolutely bonkers.

David went along with it anyway, fascinated with where his own mind was taking him. "What is the purpose of these astral planes?"

The creature snorted derisively. "What is the purpose of the earth plane? What is your purpose, for that matter?"

David could only stare at the little creature, uncomfortable at being asked that again.

"I am real, David. I look out for unusual energy signatures, for people of the earth plane who can help elevate the consciousness of the world, and I found you."

"What the actual fuck? Where is all this coming from? I've never once thought about any of this before."

"I told you, I am real."

David's heartbeat raced, and he began to lose control of the dream. Normally, he would have attempted to stay by spinning about, but he was too spooked to remain in his own head. It was getting just a little too weird for him.

He opened his eyes, blinking at the sunlight streaming through his bedroom window.

Thank God, I'm back home. That was bizarre.

It was then that he felt something on his chest. He glanced down and let out a choked gasp.

It was the creature.

David jumped to his feet. "What the fuck?"

The creature gave him a knowing look, tipped his head in acknowledgement, and ran toward the full-length mirror that sat against the wall between the TV and the study desk. It jumped into the mirror and disappeared.

Holy shit. Holy shit. Holy shit. "What the fuck just happened?"

David jumped up off his bed, grabbed his jacket, and rushed out of his bedroom, wanting to get as far away from the mirror as possible. He ran downstairs and rushed to the door, quickly opening it and heading into the fresh air.

He heard Aunt Gen shouting his name, but he ignored her and bolted away, trying to figure out what the hell had just happened.

His phone buzzed in his pocket, causing him to slow

down. He checked the text message from his friend Ronnie.

Pint?

Short but sweet and just what he needed.

His thumbs moved quickly as he replied, *When and where?*

Now and Jintys, lol

Be there in 5

Jinty McGintys in Ashton Lane was the preferred pub of choice when he and his friends met up, usually in one of the booths.

After walking in, he heard a cheer go up as his friends raised their glasses. He smiled and ambled over, giving each of his four friends — Tam, Karen, Ronnie and Aaron — a fist bump.

Ronnie motioned his eyes toward a pint sitting on the table. "Got you a lager tops mate, ya big girl's blouse."

The group of friends laughed as David picked up the pint with his right hand but grabbed it in such a way that allowed him to raise his middle finger at Ronnie. He took a gulp of his pint. Again, the group laughed.

"Touché" Ronnie quipped as he raised his glass and smiled.

David relaxed as the alcohol kicked in. He didn't

have to think about university, the argument with his aunt, and his little gargoyle friend coming into the real world.

It wasn't real.

He knew he would have to deal with it later, but he had become the master at avoidance and planned to do as much avoiding as possible.

CHAPTER 3

*G*enevieve heard the main door open as David stormed out.

"David, where are you going? We need to talk about this," she shouted as she padded through the kitchen to the front door.

It had already closed. She rolled her eyes and thought better of chasing after him. She would give him a little time to cool off.

Genevieve went upstairs and into David's room to collect his dirty washing. She didn't usually go in without his permission, but he'd left, and she needed to get things done.

A trouser leg stuck out from under the bed. Genevieve sighed and bent over to pick it up. As she pulled it out, a notebook came with it.

"Lucid Dreaming Diary 35. What's this?" She opened the book and started reading David's first entry.

November 11th, 2017

A little harder to get into a lucid dream state today. Met with the little creature again and he (it) taught me some techniques for staying in a lucid dream longer. Strange, as I am really teaching myself, so how can I know this information?

"Oh, my goodness," Genevieve whispered to herself. She looked under the bed and discovered piles of note-books. She pulled out another one and found the most recent entry. She read for another five minutes before closing it and returning it under the bed.

She looked around the room, taking it in for the first time in a long time. She was amazed to find books on lucid dreaming and astral projection.

She smiled to herself. "Why on earth didn't you tell me, David? This changes everything!"

CHAPTER 4

*A*s the day and night wore on, the group of friends became a little more obnoxious.

The drink flowed, the patrons grew in number, and live music played as a solo singer performed in the corner of the pub. The loud chatter, the laughter, and the music were too much for him. David grabbed his glass and snuck out of the booth for a quick breath of fresh air.

As he leaned his back against the whitewashed wall, he became aware of a young woman sitting at an outside table, smoking. She caught his eye and held it.

"How you doing?" she said. More of a hello than a question, but it was still polite to answer as if the question was asked.

"Good. How are you?" David replied. He noticed her long, dark hair and dark makeup, almost goth-like.

"I've had better days," she said, blowing out some smoke and looking away from David toward the pub.

He grunted and smiled. "I know what you mean."

The woman laughed. "I thought you said you were good." Her smile lit up her face, softening her whole appearance.

"Just being polite." David laughed. The woman kicked out a chair with her foot as she took another deep draw from her cigarette. Her legs were pale against the black dress and red corset top.

"I'll tell you mine, if you tell me yours." She smiled, exhaling a puff of smoke.

David accepted the invitation and smiled at her as he took his seat, setting his glass on the table. "So, what's up with you then?"

She looked at him, sizing him up. "I'm trying to make a decision about whether or not to do something I was told to do by my boss, or risk losing my job, or worse."

"Oh! Sounds like a tough position to be in. What did he ask you to do?"

"You're presuming it was a he?" She chuckled darkly. "It's actually a woman." She gazed at him thoughtfully. "You're very direct, aren't you? What age are you?"

"I'm twenty-two. Why do you ask? Are you avoiding the question?" David smiled at her, sensing this was going in another direction. She smirked.

"Yeah, I was avoiding the question. I've not decided if I should trust you."

"Quite right. You never know who you could be talking to these days," he said as he raised the half full glass to his lips. "What age are you?"

"Guess!" She leaned forward, batting her eyes in a playful gesture.

"Oh jeez, I hate this game. It never ends well. Okay, I'd say you were twenty-five."

She burst out laughing, throwing her head back. "I wish." She wiped at her eyes and smiled. "I'm thirty-two, a little too old for you, I'd say." She stood and looked down at him.

David really saw her this time. Her long dark hair contrasted starkly with her pale complexion. She didn't go for the usual trowel-on makeup and tanned look. It was natural, and it made her stand out. The corset top really was a corset, showing off her slim waist. The black, lace-like dress flowed behind her, but from the front it revealed her legs, outlining the powerful muscles in her calves and thighs.

"I have to join my friends." She caressed his cheek, giving him an enigmatic smile.

"Wait, you didn't tell me what your boss wanted you to do," David said, trying to get her to stay.

She bent over, revealing her cleavage for the first time. Placing her lips to his cheek she whispered, "My boss gave me a choice. I could fuck you, kill you, or walk away."

David raised his eyebrows in surprise and pulled back to stare at her serious expression. Her eyes drew him in.

"And what did you decide to do?"

"Well, come with me, and I'll show you." At this, she walked around the corner toward the empty car park.

David smiled to himself and followed her, thinking this was simply how she flirted.

As he rounded the corner, he looked for Goth Girl.

She'd disappeared! He turned in a circle but didn't spot her anywhere.

A great rush of energy enveloped David, lifting him into the air. He shouted in surprise as he was thrown about ten metres away, landing hard on the ground. He thanked his lucky stars there weren't any cars to break his fall. He rolled over and gingerly sat up.

He couldn't see anybody.

What the hell was that?

David heard a whooshing sound, and that same rush of energy yanked at him again, throwing him back several meters. As he hit the pavement, he spotted Goth Girl throwing her arms wide.

He cried out in pain as he was dragged along the ground. The stones and debris in the car park tore through his clothes. He looked down to see his arms dripping with blood.

Goth Girl was now walking forward, a deranged smile darkening her face.

Fuck, she's going to fucking kill me.

He jumped to his feet and charged her.

Goth Girl kept her pace, laughing at him. David felt the rage build, the full force of his shitty day breaking over him while she laughed, intent on killing him. He prepped himself to crash into her when he hit an invisible wall. The impact jarred his whole body, and he crumpled to the ground.

Witchcraft. This crazy lady was working some magic on him. Either that or he'd had way too much to drink and was just dreaming.

It doesn't feel like one of my dreams.

David lay on the ground and watched as she moved and stood over him. She held out her right hand again and twisted it. The motion somehow lifted him into the air. He tried to scream, but nothing came out. She flicked her arm, and he went slamming into one of the trees at the edge of the car park.

He heard and felt a loud crack as he landed on his arm the wrong way. The pain nauseated him.

Jeezus, this is it!

She came at him again, still laughing. As he tried to sit back up, his arm buckled, and pain shot through his spine.

"What the fuck are you doing?" David shouted as he lay on his back, not understanding what to do or why this was happening.

After a few seconds, she stood beside him again. He was too broken to move. All he could do was stare at her as she smiled.

"I told you I would show you what I had decided, and my decision was to kill you, David."

His eyes widened at the use of his name. She lifted her hand, and a small ball of flame flickered and grew just above it.

"Jeezus, what the fuck is this? This has to be a dream."

David looked for signs, anything that would clue him in. He had to wake up. His heart sank as he found a sign on the side of the building and realised, he could read it. "Oh fuck, this is not good."

Goth Girl raised her arm, closing her eyes as if summoning something. She drew her arm back, ready to launch her fireball, when someone else appeared just between him and Goth Girl.

She had long, red hair that flowed past her shoulders. She wore a camouflage jumpsuit and stood with her hands on her hips. He wanted to warn her to get the hell out of there, but before he could, she lifted her hand and blew Goth Girl a kiss. The witch flew back about twenty feet, screaming the entire way, and suddenly winked out of existence.

David looked around. There was no one else in the car park but himself and the redhead now.

I have to be dreaming. This must be a dream.

The young woman walked over to him.

"Are you okay?" She bent low, offering David her hand.

He reached for it, but pain tore through his body as

she pulled. He gasped as his vision grew dark from the agony. She stopped pulling and bent down, examining his injuries.

"Broken," she muttered. "Arm. A few ribs. Possibly your hip. What a heinous bitch she was."

"I honestly haven't a clue what's going on. I...I don't know..."

She laughed. "It's okay. I'll explain. My name is Jessica, or Jess to my friends, and it's nice to finally meet you, David. I'll shake your hand once we get you fixed up."

CHAPTER 5

*D*avid was silent as he walked next to the young woman who had introduced herself as Jessica, the woman who had saved his ass and healed him in the process.

They were headed to his house. Jessica had insisted on accompanying him home. He felt like an idiot, being protected by a girl. Sounded sexist, but he still felt stupid. They continued to walk to David's home in silence for what seemed like an age as he processed what had happened back in the car park.

Jessica looked at him and smiled a few times but gave him the space he needed.

"How do you know my name?" he said, finally breaking the silence.

"I know Genevieve Hunter, and we are aware of your energy in the dreaming or astral world," Jessica said.

"Wait, you know my Aunt Gen? How?" David asked.

"I think it's better if your aunt and I explain a few things to you. I presume we're going to your Aunt Genevieve's house?"

"Yeah," David said, shaking his head, still unable to process everything that was going on. He had confidently established that this was not a dream, but he just couldn't fathom what else it could be.

Jessica laid her hand on his arm. "It will all become clear when we get to your aunt's house. I know how weird this all seems just now."

"Just a tad weird, yeah," David said. "Ah, thanks for saving me back there. You know. I had it under control, of course, but it was nice of you to help."

Jessica chuckled but didn't comment.

As they neared the house, he could see his Aunt Gen looking out of her bay window as she paced up and down.

She must be really upset that I left.

David inwardly cringed when she spotted them, but instead of the irate expression he expected, she appeared relieved. She beckoned them through the window.

The door opened before they got to the bottom of the steps. "David, thank goodness you're okay. I had a horrible feeling something had happened." She then looked at Jessica and did a double take when recognition kicked in. "Jessica Campbell? Oh, my goodness, it's been a while. What on earth are you doing here?"

David looked at both of them. "And how on earth do you two know each other?" he asked.

"Come on in and get warmed up. I'll put the kettle on for some tea. We've got a lot to talk about."

Aunt Gen led them into the living room. David studied his aunt's interactions with Jessica. It was obvious they had known each other for a long time. So why had he never met her?

Feeling exhausted, he sank into the brown leather sofa as Aunt Gen and Jessica made tea in the kitchen. He went over everything that had happened that day, trying to make sense of it all, but there was just no getting his head around anything.

Aunt Gen came through and set a tray down on the small table. It had a large teapot, three cups, and a plate of biscuits.

Jessica sat on the armchair next to David, and his Aunt Gen sat on the Chesterfield opposite him.

"Jessica filled me in on what happened. Extremely troubling, but we'll get to that in a minute. Now, I'm sure you have a million questions, but I have to start by apologising for today."

David looked at his aunt in bewilderment.

She's apologising when I'm the one close to expulsion? What the hell?

She looked at Jessica. "I know we have a guest, and I don't want to get too deep into the university issue, but I shouldn't have behaved the way I did, and I apologise."

"No, honestly. I've been acting like a spoiled brat, and today I went over the top."

"We can talk about it later. I think there's more pressing matters at hand just now."

David raised his eyebrows and looked at both women. "I'd say so."

"First of all, I want to know why you were attacked. I need to ask you if anything strange has happened recently?"

"Nearly being killed tonight isn't strange enough?"

"You're lucid dreaming, David. Has anything strange happened in your dreams?"

"How do you know about that?"

His aunt just stared at him. He let out a weary sigh. "Define strange. There have been varying degrees of it."

"Let's start with what happened tonight," Jessica said.

He thought back to the creature today. "Maybe some background first. I've been lucid dreaming for ages, well, years..." He paused. "How much do you know about lucid dreaming, Auntie?"

Jessica and Aunt Gen looked at each other and burst out laughing.

"We're quite familiar with it, child. Continue."

He shrugged and kept going, deciding nothing could shock him after what had happened to him tonight. "When I lucid dream, I have this little creature friend who visits me."

"Gargoyle?" Jessica asked.

"Why do you know this?" David shook his head. "You know what? Never mind. I'm just gonna get this out. Today, the creature..." He paused, thinking it still sounded crazy. "He came into the real world from my dream and disappeared into my bedroom mirror. How's that for strange?" He let out a sigh. It felt good to talk about it even if it was crazy.

Jessica and Aunt Gen looked at each other and nodded like they understood. Like gargoyles appearing from dreams and jumping into mirrors was completely within the realm of normal.

"That explains it," they said in unison.

"What? That explains what?" David asked, frustrated.

"The woman who tried to kill you in the car park must have picked up on the energy spike when the creature crossed from the dream world into the earth plane. You were identified and tracked," Jessica said, as if it was an everyday occurrence.

That thought jarred David's mind again, the fact that someone was actually trying to kill him.

"Right. About that. Why was she trying to kill me, and how did you know to stop her?"

It was as if he'd spoken to the wind. Aunt Gen and Jessica completely ignored his questions and changed the subject.

"I didn't have any inclination at all that you had the gift or the interest in the astral planes, or we would have been having this conversation years ago." She poured a cup of tea and continued speaking about astral planes as if it was normal.

David tried to steer the conversation back to the issue at hand. "Okay, I'm not getting it at all. How can people do magic in car parks and disappear and reappear out of thin air? How did that little creature come into the real world from the dream world? How do you even know about any of this, Aunt Gen? Am I missing something, or am I really going nuts?"

"Okay, I think we should start from the beginning," Aunt Gen said.

"That's a good place to start," David said.

"You're a dream dancer. Someone who can travel the astral world and someone who has...certain powers, shall we say. A dream dancer is a certain race of witch, and lucid dreaming is a branch of witchcraft, a specialisation if you like." Aunt Gen paused to look at him.

"I'm a witch? Is that what you're saying?" David asked, not liking the sound of it.

"Well, you're not a witch. Technically, you're a wizard. Well, we think you are. We'll need to get The Glowing Ceremony organised to test you, but that's for another time."

"I can do magick?" David asked, looking between Jessica and Aunt Gen.

"Yes," they said.

"Have you heard of the Golden Triangle?"

David looked at her and frowned, shaking his head. "What is it?"

"It's an area in Glasgow's West End that is a property hotspot. It runs from Highburgh Road, to Hyndland Road, up to Great Western Road, and down Byers Road. So, all the roads and streets within this area is known as the Golden Triangle. Of course, estate agents have referred to this as a property hotspot..." She shifted in her seat, looked at David, and took a deep breath. "...but the origins of it have nothing to do with property. It's to do with energy. Edinburgh has a golden triangle as well."

"Energy? What do you mean? I don't get you."

She looked out the window and took another sip of her tea. "It's an area where there is more magickal energy. Energy where magick can be performed more easily. Energy where we can cross other worlds more easily. It's just a magickal, mystical, beautiful type of energy, untouched by evil and protected by good forces."

David's jaw dropped at that. He couldn't speak; he just looked at her.

Is my Aunt Gen actually speaking these words?

"There's quite a lot to know. Suffice it to say, I think that's why you've been experiencing some strange occurrences recently. Your energy is maturing, although God knows how." She looked him up and down. "But you're resonating at a similar energy and tapping into the power grid, so to speak. Lucid dreaming is the start of something much bigger.'"

Jessica watched him. He felt her measuring his every reaction.

"There's going to be big changes, David. Changes that you might not want to make, but it will be your decision as to whether you want to make those changes after the Glowing," Jessica said.

"Okay. What's the Glowing?"

"It's where we find out what level of dream dancer you are. There are seven levels. Actually, there are ten, but seven main levels which correspond to the seven planes of existence. There's lots to learn, but I'm giving you the main points." Jessica took a sip of her tea and continued. "Depending on how strong your inner energy is, you'll be able to travel to these different levels. Most dream dancers are emotionals, casuals, or mentals which are second and third plane travellers."

"What's the point of being able to travel the different planes?"

"There is no point. It's just an ability you're born with, usually passed down through the generations via the genes," Jessica said.

"We thought it had skipped a generation with you, which is why you haven't been told anything about it until now." Aunt Gen offered him a smile that said she was actually proud of him.

"So, The Glowing is something that will tell me if I have the power or not?"

"Not the power, the energy, yes. Don't mistake

having the energy as having power. Yes, it is a power, but it's really about the energy."

"Okay, what can I do if I have the energy?" David said, leaning forward on the sofa.

"You can travel to the different planes with astral projection, and you can manipulate energy on the earth plane, as you saw tonight when I appeared out of nowhere. Obviously, if you have this energy control, there's other things you can do, BUT there's always a cause and effect. So, for example, if you kill someone, then someone you love will most likely be killed. You might even be killed," Jessica said.

"Right, I get all that Karma stuff, but I still don't understand why we have the pow...sorry, energy."

"Evolution. You are here to help with the evolution of humanity," Aunt Gen chimed in.

"How am I going to help with evolution? I mean, we've only been evolving for millions of years. How can we help?" David asked, laughing.

His Aunt Gen thought about it for a few seconds. "How do we evolve, David? As a race, how have we evolved? We've gone from the larvae in the swamps of the world, to swimming in the deepest of oceans, to crawling on land, then walking, then making fire, then thinking, then creating. All of that is only possible if we oscillate at a different energy." She spoke a little quicker now, with a little more excitement. David could tell she was passionate about this. "The energy of *homo erectus* would differ greatly from the energy frequency of *homo sapiens.*" She paused and looked at him. "You are the next stage of human evolution." Aunt Gen stopped and took another sip of her tea.

"Whoa, that's a lot to take in..."

"That's just the tip of the iceberg. However, fascinating as that may be, the more pressing matter is the de-evolution of mankind."

"De-evolution. How can you de-evolve?" David laughed at the absurdity of this.

"By lowering the energy of the entire human race." Aunt Gen stared intently at David.

"Well, that's not possible. How can we lower the energy of seven and a half billion people?"

Aunt Gen's smile conveyed pity. "Media, in all its forms; news, radio, TV, social media, newspapers, the internet, movies, TV series. This is how they lower the energy of the human race."

"Who's they?"

"The government, the people in power, and secret organisations."

David laughed again and looked at Jessica and Aunt Gen for signs of this being a joke.

This all sounds like a conspiracy theory.

Of course, he'd nearly been killed by a witch, so anything was possible.

Jessica and Aunt Gen certainly weren't laughing. They were serious.

Jessica put her cup down on the table and gave David a stern look. "If you can control the energy of the population, then you can control the evolution of the population. The people who are doing the controlling want people like you, me, and your Aunt Gen dead. There is a whole community of witches, wizards, dream dancers and the rest of the weird fringe dwellers that exist, and these organisations, some of them government controlled, will stop at nothing to retain their power and their control over the minds and energies of billions of people, especially when some of them are supernatural like us."

"Do we know who these people are?"

"We know of a few smaller ones, but the ones who run the show, well, we don't know them yet, and we're constantly working to find out who they are." Jessica paused again and glanced at Aunt Gen. "Does he know about his parents?"

David widened his eyes in disbelief. Irritation and annoyance pricked at him. He knew nothing about them, and this strange girl had answers?

"Has my being attacked got something to do with my mum and dad leaving me with you?" He looked directly at his Aunt Gen, who appeared to be thinking about the question.

"I know how deeply this has hurt you and affected you, David, but you have to trust me when I say that your mother and father didn't abandon you."

"You keep saying that, but you never tell me anything else," David said, almost pleading.

Aunt Gen shook her head. "I will make you a promise. When the time is right, you will know everything concerning your parents. Please, trust me, David."

David shrugged his shoulders, feeling resigned.

She's trying to protect me. There's obviously a lot more to this. How could any parent just abandon their child and never see them again?

He decided it would be best to drop the subject and never bring it up again. After all, what good would it possibly do to know at this point?

CHAPTER 6

$\mathcal{A}$licia Collins looked over the bannisters and down towards the bottom of the fifty-two-storey building. The glass atrium housed the largest indoor park in the world with hundreds of different species of plants and trees. It dwarfed the Ford Foundations building on 43rd Street.

Alicia smiled as she surveyed her kingdom. AICILA Media Inc. was named after her, with a little twist by spelling her name backwards, and left to her when her father had died five years ago under suspicious circumstances. Nothing had ever come of the investigations, and Alicia had been too devastated to keep the investigation going.

She glanced at her watch. 1pm. The meeting would start in fifteen minutes.

As she sat down and shuffled her seat under the

desk, she clicked the mouse to reopen the file she'd been perusing.

We conclude that the killing of the three scientists in Budapest was carried out by an Essential or higher. The abilities demonstrated originated from someone adept and well trained. Although, at this time, the Essential is an unknown person to us, we are following up some leads in Scotland, England, France, and Russia. The report on these leads will be with you shortly and then updated on a daily basis.

Alicia ran her fingers through her shoulder-length hair and mentally prepared herself for the meeting. Her papers were laid out in front of her, the spreadsheet was open on the computer, and her coffee was piping hot. She was all set to go.

These types of meetings were always in person, and everyone was scanned for recording equipment. All phones and pens were confiscated. It was an ultra-secure environment, and anybody who betrayed the trust of Alicia Collins was dealt with, although it had only happened twice in the last five years. Those individuals were now dead.

Within fifteen minutes, everyone had assembled, and the meeting began.

A silver-haired man with a goatee and a blue Armani suit cleared his throat as he prepared to speak. "We have no further updates on the dream dancers we are following. There's been no suspicious activity from any of them, although, getting close to them is proving a little more difficult due to their abilities."

Alicia listened carefully. "Do we have any real suspicions, or are we grasping at straws here?"

The silver-haired man took a deep breath and opened his palms toward Alicia. "Possibly. The dream dancer from Scotland is most suspicious just now, but inside sources are yet to confirm her involvement."

"Kill her!" Alicia stared him square in the eyes with no hint of anything except a "just do it" look.

A hush engulfed the room.

The man spoke a little more slowly, "We can't...just kill her, Ms. Collins. She's connected, and she is possibly an Essential or higher. That's just asking for trouble." He looked at her, waiting for a reaction.

She stood and placed her hands on the desk, leaning on the table towards the man. "First, we can do anything we fucking want to do, and second, don't presume to know me well enough to be my advisor. I don't need or want your fucking advice. I want facts and action. Is that clear?"

The silver-haired man's cheeks reddened, either with anger or embarrassment. He nodded slightly, still looking her in the eyes.

"Well?" She said.

"Yes, Ms. Collins, that is very clear." He said it through clenched teeth.

She continued to stare at the man until he looked away. Suddenly changing her demeanour, Alicia cheerfully blurted out, "Now! Where are we with the new batch of the virus?"

A woman at the bottom of the table quickly replied, "The virus has been tested and should be ready within the next two months; everything is ahead of schedule just now."

"And where are the labs for this virus?"

The woman shook her head, narrowing her eyes. "Em...nobody knows where the labs are, under your orders, Ms. Collins."

Alicia smiled. "Good. Everything is on track. Now, do we have any new measurement scores for the energy around the world?"

Jean-Luc Tisserand glanced at Alicia and then focused on the sheet of paper in front of him. His deep French accent boomed around the room. "Yes, Ms. Collins. Our data miners through social media indicate the recent political unrest around the world is having a significant effect on the energy levels of the people. Rioting in America is on all international news channels, the French police have been lambasted for their handling of the recent protests, Germany has seen much the same, and the UK... well, the UK have their prime minister who is a one-man show of unrest." There was a smile from Alicia and some laughter from others around the table. "The rest of Europe continues to slip into economic decline. It's all contributing to the 'E' number going down ten points on a global scale."

Alicia nodded and smiled, encouraging him to continue.

"I believe if we can release the virus in the next four months, the twenty-two-year cycle of energy upgrading will be delayed. This will allow us the time and energy to work on The Akashic Records."

"Good." Alicia folded her arms. *It's all going as planned* she thought. "Okay, let's continue."

The meeting carried on with reports of AICILA Media Inc. being more in control of the news and media throughout the world with newspaper and media buyouts, some legal issues with government bodies over possible monopolisation issues, and the crashing of the cryptocurrency market in order to buy it up and control it. AICILA Media now had over 2.1 million Bitcoin and could control the market at will, meaning they would never be short of funds, ever.

After three hours, the meeting ended, and as usual, Alicia invited her most trusted confidantes to stay behind and discuss things further. There was Zhao Wei, a Chinese news reporter, Gordon Truby, a Wall Street financial analyst and advisor, James Yorke, an English MP and close friend to the current prime minister and possibly future prime minister, and Barbara Kruger, a German political analyst to discuss things further.

They were relaxed in each other's company and could speak their minds.

Alicia offered them all a glass of whisky which she poured deftly from the ornate wide neck decanter sitting on the elegant marble coffee table. She sat back and regarded them coolly before addressing them.

"We found out today that the Galaxy Bridge Media deal will be going through within the next eight weeks, so we will be the proud owners of one of the biggest media companies in the world. AT&T will receive over 100 billion dollars for the deal, and we will be nabbing what is commonly known as a bargain. Our assets will be worth over one trillion dollars once the deal is signed. Here's to power and control." She held up her glass.

"To power and control." The rest of the group lifted their glasses and laughed.

Alicia crossed her legs and draped her arm over the back of the sofa. Her Balmain stretch-knit midi dress hugged her slim figure. She looked at the others as she sipped her whisky.

She smiled as she thought about the promise she had made to her eleven-year-old self all those years ago.

Never again will anyone have any control over me. I will control my future.

CHAPTER 7

*D*avid had gone to bed replaying the events of the last twenty-four hours. For the first time in his life, he felt there was a brighter future for him. Yet somehow, it was going to be even more difficult. The hope was enough to carry him through.

He thought back to everything that had happened. The magical world of witches and dream dancers excited and terrified him. The creature from his dreams materialising in real life made him wonder about other creatures out there. Then he thought about his new friend Jess and how she'd saved his life. And to top it off, Aunt Gen was a witch, or a dream dancer, or both.

As he walked downstairs, he heard chatter from the kitchen. Aunt Gen and Jessica, who had stayed last night, were discussing the events of the day before and planning his Glowing Ceremony when David walked into the kitchen.

"Morning!" He looked at Jess and smiled at Aunt Gen.

"Good morning, my little dream dancer, how did you sleep?" Aunt Gen said jovially.

"I slept very well, eventually, once I got my head around everything that's happened over the last few days," he said.

Jessica smiled. "We're just organising your Glowing Ceremony. We need to do it as quickly as possible and start your training."

"My training?" asked David.

"Oh yeah. You didn't think you'd have access to all that magick without any training, did you?" Jessica asked.

"Well, I kinda did, actually."

Jessica and Aunt Gen laughed. "That would be like expecting to get your law degree in a day just because you had the capability to study." Jessica laughed at the absurdity of this.

"Oh great, gotta do more studying. Yay, fantastic," David said, giving them a thumbs up and twisting his face in mock enthusiasm.

"Your life is never going to be the same again," Jessica said.

David excitedly rubbed his hands together. "Okay, when do I start the training?"

"Here's your first part of the training." Jess looked at Aunt Gen and laughed. "Go take a freezing cold shower."

"What?" David said, sitting back. "Why a freezing cold shower?"

"You have to train yourself to be in control. You have a little voice in your head that tends to take over, causing you to procrastinate on studying, eating whatever you want, not going to the gym, doing all the things that are easy to do. That's a little devil sitting inside its wee comfort zone controlling you."

"Okay," David said slowly.

"Well, you have to take back control. Demonstrate some willpower," Jess said.

Aunt Gen listened with interest. "I'd love to see that."

"Can't I do something else?" David hated the thought of a cold shower.

Jessica laughed. "Okay, David, stand on that chair for five minutes."

"What? Just stand on the chair?" David said, frowning.

"Yes, that's it."

David got up from the chair he sat on and held onto the back as he stepped onto its seat. He crossed his arms as he stood, looking a little smug at first. After about one minute he said, "This is silly."

"Keep standing," Jess said.

"Okay, what's the point of this? I just look ridiculous," David said, putting his hands in his pockets.

"Oh my god, it's only been two minutes, keep standing," Jess said, looking at her watch.

After three minutes, David stepped from the chair and sat back down. "I don't get it. What is the point of doing that?"

"Because, that little voice inside your head is controlling you, saying things like, this is silly, I look ridiculous, they're just laughing at me, and I look like a fool. All because it's outside its comfort zone, and all it wants to do is go back to its comfort zone. That's the control it has over you."

"But I *am* in control. I came down from the chair after three minutes," David said, narrowing his eyes as he tried to understand.

"That wasn't you. You're so used to being controlled; you think that voice is yours. Go on, try it again. This time it's YOU who is in control," Jess said, challenging him.

"Okay." David once again got up and stood on the chair.

He kept his position for five minutes, on the chair, in silence, trying not to move a muscle. After Jess indicated that time was up, he jumped down.

"Jeez, that was a lot more difficult than I thought it would be," David said.

Aunt Gen laughed at them as she carried on making breakfast.

"Did you hear all the excuses the little voice made for you?"

"I did. It didn't stop talking."

"So how did you do it?" Jess asked.

"I told it I was in charge, and I was going to stand there for five minutes." David suddenly stopped. "Ah, I get it," he said slowly.

"You see? There's two voices: you, although your voice is usually in the background, and the little devil's voice controlling you without you knowing it."

Aunt Gen turned to Jess. "That's actually a great way of explaining it. You're good at this, Jessica." She handed Jess a plate and dished out some eggs, bacon, black pudding, mushrooms, haggis, and beans.

"Oh, a full Scottish breakfast. I love it," David said, as Aunt Gen passed his plate over to him.

"Now, the next part of your training is to not eat that breakfast and give it to me," Jess said, smiling.

"Not a chance. I'll let the wee devil stay in control of this one." David cut a piece of black pudding and smeared it on some toast. He closed his eyes. "Heaven on a plate."

Aunt Gen and Jess smiled at him as they ate their breakfast in silence. After they had finished their breakfast and washed up, they headed upstairs for the first part of his training. Apparently, the cold shower was not optional.

David went into the en-suite with Jess waiting for him in the bedroom. "This is ridiculous. I can't believe I'm actually doing this." David pulled off all of his clothes and then turned the shower to its lowest setting. "I hope you're not taking the piss, Jess." He heard her laughing as she sat on his bed.

He felt the freezing spray hit his legs before he even got in the shower. He let out an involuntary yelp.

Jess shouted, "Just get in, you big woos."

"Yeah, yeah. Alright for you to say. I bet you don't have cold showers."

"I have one every morning. Now get in there!" She laughed when he grumbled back at her.

"Right, I'm going for it." He went to step in and jerked back. He braced himself again and this time walked straight in, sticking himself directly under the showerhead. "Jeezus. Jeezus." He took deep breaths in. "Ah!" He heard Jess laughing. "Not...funny," he said, taking another deep breath in.

He managed to stay in the shower for over five minutes. After quickly drying himself off, his skin had patches of red from the freezing water. Quickly flinging on his jeans and t-shirt, he went out into his bedroom where Jess looked through some of his albums. She turned around.

"God, you're such a big girl's blouse." She laughed.

"How often do I have to have cold showers?"

"Every day from now on." She gave him a teasing grin. "There are lots of benefits to cold showers."

"Yeah, I'm sure there are. I'm not feeling any benefits just now," he said, still shivering. "When do we get to the good stuff when it comes to training?"

"Trust me, there's a lot to do before you can even begin to travel to level one. I promise it will all be worth it."

"Listen Jess, I really appreciate you taking the time to help me."

"No problem, but I have ulterior motives. You can be part of my PhD paper. It's about NDEs and OBEs, so you are a perfect case study for this. Think of me spending time with you as part of my research."

David looked at her. "NDEs, OBEs?"

"Oh, Out of Body Experiences and Near-Death Experiences," Jess said.

David grinned. "Using me, are you? I don't know if I like the sound of that. Come to think of it, I do like the sound of that." His smile turned flirtatious.

"Men, you're all the same." Jess laughed. She sat on his desk chair and got down to business. "Okay, so here's a list of things you'll need to change to better control your mind. The cool part about this is doing these things will help with every other aspect of your life. You ready?"

"I'm ready," David said, listening as he leant forward on the bed.

"Where's your notepad? You'll need to write this down." Jess looked a little horrified that David hadn't even considered taking notes.

"Oh, of course." He leaped forward and scrambled about in his desk drawer. "Got one," he said, sitting back down.

Jess looked at him expectantly. When David didn't respond, she sighed in exasperation. "Pen!"

"Oh, of course." He went back and grabbed a pen from the desktop.

"This is going to be tough training you," Jess joked. "Okay, every day you need to do these things. One: cold shower every morning. Two: keep a journal and write in it every day. Three —"

"Keep a journal? Why do I need to keep a journal?" He didn't have a problem with it since he had his own dream journals, but he wondered at her reasoning.

Jess threw her hands in the air. "David, it's all to do with discipline. You need to take control of every aspect of your life and doing things like this will train your brain. You form good habits and keep them, instilling a sense of discipline. It's going to help you focus, and it's going to make you more determined. You need all these if you're ever going to be able to practise astral projection. The ability to astral project is all about focus and discipline. If you aren't in control of your mind, then you'll never gain mastery over this." Jess raised her eyebrows as if daring him to challenge her further.

"Okay, okay. I get it. Carry on."

Jess shook her head. "Three: go walking, jogging, or get in a good workout at the gym every day. Physical activity lends strength to mental fortitude, and pushing your body has a lot to do with mastery over mind. If you must have a day off, then do so on a Sunday, but the rest of the week must be dedicated to training your body and mind. At least thirty to sixty minutes of exercise. This will keep your body fit so it doesn't let you down when you're using your mind to astral travel. Remember, your mind can't differentiate between the astral world and the physical world. For all intents and purposes, the astral world is just another physical world. Does that make sense?"

"Kinda, yeah," David said as he jotted some notes down.

"Good. Four: drink at least four litres of water every day. Your energy output and energy absorption depend on what you eat and your intake of fluids. Water balances your energies which is crucial for astral travel."

"What, four litres of water, I barely drink half a litre just now. That's a lot of water." David exclaimed.

"It is but trust me you need it," Jessica said. "And five: this is a tricky one, but you need to start facing all your fears and phobias if you have any."

David looked at her in surprise. "All my fears and phobias?"

"As many as you possibly can. Do you suffer from any at the moment?"

"How long have you got? I could name a hundred things off the top of my head."

"What are your biggest fears?" Jess asked.

"I don't like heights, spiders, snakes, roller coasters, flying, Pierrot dolls —"

"Wait, what? Pierrot dolls?"

"Yeah, they're creepy as fuck," David said, his eyes wide.

Jess laughed. "Okay I think we have enough to get you started. You need to face your fears on this plane before you face what's on the next level, and believe me, there's a lot of things that will scare you on all the different planes of existence."

"Oh, you're not going to make me hold spiders and shit like that, are you?"

"I'm afraid so. You have to do it. Any break in concentration or shock to the system elevates heart rate and jolts your focus. Losing that in the middle of astral travel is dangerous depending on what you're doing at the time. Honestly, you'll get to the point where you fear nothing."

"This is not sounding quite as exciting as it did a few hours ago."

Jessica's smirk said it all. "David, you have to believe me when I tell you, your life is going to be unrecognisable in a few months. You're not going to be the same man, so enjoy this while you can. Also, your aunt wants to speak to you about meeting someone important."

"Now?" David asked.

Jess checked her watch. "Yeah, we should probably get down there."

Both Jess and David went downstairs and joined his aunt in the kitchen. She pottered about, looking flustered with excitement.

"Have you two finished larking around? I heard you laughing from down here," Gen said, although she wore a smile.

"Sorry, Aunt Gen, I was freezing my nuts...er...oops, freezing myself to death with that cold shower."

"I liked it. I miss the sound of laughter." She looked out the window as she placed some plates on the rack.

Jess walked toward Aunt Gen. "I've told David you want him to meet someone."

"Oh yes." Aunt Gen dried her hands with a nearby dishcloth. "Everyone who goes through The Glowing Ceremony, and has accepted the path of the Dream Dancer, goes to visit a seer. This is someone who feels and senses your path and where it will lead you. You can go with a friend, family member, or go on your own. It's up to you."

"What kind of things will they say? I mean, what did they say to you?" he asked his Aunt Gen.

"I was told I was a mediator, and my strengths lay in teaching, communicating, and keeping the peace. I didn't take much heed at first, but it turns out the seer was right. It's what I've done most of my life."

David turned to Jess. "What did they tell you?"

Jess looked at Aunt Gen and back to David. "I was told I would lead. I'd be a light on the path for others, a warrior in the field of battle."

"A warrior?" David thought about it. "You were definitely one last night when you saved me from that woman. Is there really an active battle going on, though?"

"Oh yes," Jess said. "More than you realise, David. You might be told the path is not for you, or you might be told you're the general meant to lead the battle. Nobody knows until they speak to a seer, and it's not always something an individual actually becomes."

"So, you mean I might not be a dream dancer at the end of this, even after The Glowing Ceremony?"

Aunt Gen looked at him and shook her head. "No, that's not what we are saying." She thought for a second and looked around the room. "Okay, that lightbulb is not on yet, and won't light this room unless we switch it on. It has to be wired correctly for it to work. It has what is known as potential energy. You are that light. You have the frequency of energy required to travel the different astral planes, but you need the right training, the right conditions, and the right mindset and mental toughness to do that. What you have at the moment is potential. If you decide to sit on your backside and do nothing with that potential, nothing will happen. You won't travel the seven planes or help elevate the energy of others in the world, and you will not light the path of the dream dancer for others, BUT you have the potential."

"Ah, okay. I get it," said David, nodding his head. "What is the seer going to tell me then?"

"Basically, how big a role being a dream dancer is going to play in your life. You might decide not to follow the path, and that would be that. Nothing more would happen."

"So, when do I get to visit with the seer?"

"There is one in Edinburgh. We can contact her and set up an appointment."

"Okay, back to The Glowing. When will that happen?"

"I've got people coming around today, but we should plan and organise within a few days. Jess, I presume you will be there?" asked Aunt Gen.

"Definitely. I wouldn't miss it," Jess said with a smile.

CHAPTER 8

*G*enevieve Hunter's excitement increased as she considered David's upcoming ceremony.

She could see him transitioning, a little later than most, but the transition seemed latent with power. She suspected David would surprise them all, but she would have to wait for The Glowing.

The kitchen table was laden with cakes, three teapots, some scones, and strawberry jam and butter.

The doorbell signalled the first of her ten guests. It was Rodrigo from Westbourne Gardens. After they had exchanged a hug and some pleasantries, he took his seat at the table, buttered a scone, and poured himself a cup of tea.

The rest of the guests arrived within ten minutes of each other. Not surprising since they were all within walking distance of each other. Gen appreciated their punctuality as she abhorred tardiness.

Sitting at the head of the table, she scanned the room, studying her friends as they chatted with one another. Gen knew things were going to change. She felt a pang of sadness. David's transitioning meant she would take on the role of part mentor to David, if he chose to take up the call.

Gen thought back to her own Glowing and how nervous she had been. She'd been brought up with magick all her life, and it was all she knew. She had learned to hide it well from the outside world.

Her thoughts were brought back to the present as the noise around the table trickled to a low hum. They now looked to Gen to start the proceedings.

She looked around the table, each face a member of the Glasgow Board of Dream Dancers. Without preamble, she stated her reason for calling their meeting together.

"David, it would seem, is in a transitioning phase. I recently learned he has been practising lucid dreaming without my knowledge." There were a few shocked looks, but they were followed quickly with smiles and nods of approval. Everyone had assumed that the magick had skipped a generation. "I don't know how powerful he is, if he is powerful at all, and I haven't the foggiest notion about his abilities. So, I am here to ask permission to set a date for The Glowing, but we need it to happen as quickly as possible, preferably tomorrow."

"Did something happen?" one woman in the group asked.

"Yes, he was attacked last night by another dream dancer, and it was only through Jessica Campbell's quick interference that he survived. If you all recall, she's Joseph Campbell's daughter."

A noise of shock and excited chatter rose in the room as the energy picked up. Dream dancers attacking others wasn't unheard of, but it didn't happen very often. Unfortunately, there were some dream dancers who didn't see the evolution of humans as a good thing.

The thought of another member joining the Golden Triangle branch was exciting to the board, and of course, there was The Glowing. It would be the talk of the country if David turned out to be as high as an Essential, but it was highly unlikely as the energy of most dream dancers follow the mother's line, and Gen herself was a Causal, a higher third-plane dream dancer.

One man from the group leaned forward. "Have you discussed this with David yet? He needs to know what's involved."

"I have given him the basic information, but that is all. I think he had enough to try and wrap his head around."

"That he was attacked is odd. These acts of violence usually happen to powerful dream dancers who are viewed as a threat. He shouldn't have been on anyone's radar. Has there been anything strange happening Gen?" The speaker was another woman with long dark hair and a soft voice.

Gen looked at the faces around the table and hesitated. "I didn't let on to David at the time, but from what he described to me, it sounds as if he pulled a Watcher back from the lucid world."

Shocked silence met her reply.

"That means his energy must be extremely high. That's a difficult thing to do intentionally let alone accidentally," the soft-spoken woman said.

"Oh, my goodness, is that not the sign of a Manifestal? This is incredible," Rodrigo said.

Pockets of conversations broke out as board members discussed this new information and worried as to David being a target.

"Why didn't you say anything when you called us?" Rodrigo finally said above the din.

"I didn't want to alarm you or get you too excited. There is much we don't know, and speculation is fruitless. We've seen this happen before with novices, and it's always turned out to be accidental. Listen, there is no point in getting ahead of ourselves until The Glowing determines David's energy levels and potential. It is of paramount importance that he learns to protect himself. So, we need to set a date and appoint the ceremony leader."

It was agreed that The Glowing Ceremony should happen in two days, enough time to fill David in on more information and let him know what to expect. This would be so foreign to him, and it would take him some time to adjust to a new world with new rules. Gen wondered if he might decide not to follow the path of the dream dancer.

After spending a few hours going over the recent developments and other pressing business, everyone said their goodbyes and went their separate ways. Only Gwen remained behind, someone who had been best friends with Aunt Gen since childhood.

As Gwen and Gen retired to the drawing room, they looked at each other and started to laugh. It was filled with excitement, a laugh to acknowledge something new and wonderful had happened.

"A wee sherry for the road, Gwen?"

"Oh, go on then." Gwen laughed. As she sipped her VORS Sherry, she took on a more serious tone. "Gen, have you thought about the implications of David being an Essential, or maybe higher?"

Gen raised a pensive brow before speaking. "I have. I know we are excited at the prospect of David being an Essential, but it does bring with it a lot of potential problems, not just for David, but for the entire board. We may even have to take it to the Scottish Board or even the British Board. He'll have a target on his back, but to be honest, I think he already does." Gen looked into the distance, not relishing the thought of having to register David and the attention this would bring.

"We could skip The Glowing, you know. There's no law that says it has to be completed. All David has done is tell you that he practises lucid dreaming," Gwen said, taking another sip of her Sherry. Her long blonde hair fell across her shoulder as she shifted in her seat.

"I did think about that as well." With another smile and that hint of cheekiness in her eyes, Gen said, "I'm excited to see if he really is a dream dancer, even if he is a Physical or an Etheric." She laughed and held out her glass to Gwen. "A little toast to David and whatever type of DD he is."

"To David." Gwen smiled, chinking glasses with Gen.

CHAPTER 9

*D*avid's nerves grew as The Glowing drew near. On the day of his ceremony, Jess travelled over from Edinburgh to be in the gathering, and her father had sent his best wishes for him.

There were around thirty people due to arrive at Aunt Gen's house. Jess and David helped rearrange the furniture in the drawing room to accommodate all the guests. It now looked huge to David, as the antique whisky chesterfields were pushed back to the sides of the room, and the mahogany coffee tables had been placed in the two corners with large velvet cushions on top to offer more seating.

Neither Jess nor his Aunt Gen had told him what to expect for fear that it might somehow skew the outcome, or at least that's what they had told David.

He looked at his phone to note the time. Only 1:33pm. Jess noticed his anxiousness and laughed.

"Oh my god, I haven't seen anyone as nervous as this," she said, flicking back her long red hair.

David looked at her and took a deep breath in. "I have to admit I am nervous." He looked out of the bay window onto the street below. "Okay, I'm going out for a run."

"No!" Jess and his Aunt Gen cried in unison.

"You want to have as much energy as possible for The Glowing. Going for a run will only deplete it," his Aunt Gen explained.

Jess walked over to David and linked her arm with his. "C'mon, let's go watch something mindless on Netflix, something you don't have to think too much about, and we can preserve your energy."

He was aware of her presence as she linked her arm through his. He loved her company and didn't want to spoil the friendship that was developing between them by thinking it could be anything more.

David and Jess spent the afternoon in the drawing room talking, watching TV, eating. Of course, they were both killing time until The Glowing started, but it was a beautiful way to kill time.

At around 4pm, the first of the guests arrived, and Aunt Gen was in her element. She loved entertaining and was proud of her home and the energy it gave off.

David and Jess were introduced to a gentleman who spoke with an accent David couldn't place. He had to tilt his head back to look him in the eye, which meant he was much taller than David's six-foot frame. The gentleman was delighted to meet Jess. He knew her father well and had heard all about her. Jess smiled politely.

The same thing happened with all the other guests. All of them knew Joseph Campbell and were delighted to meet Jess, delighted to be invited to David's Glowing Ceremony, and delighted it was being hosted at Aunt Gen's.

Lots of delighted individuals.

Aunt Gen made sure guests had coffee and tea — or something a little stronger for those in need — and directed everyone's attention to the buffet in the dining room.

She looked a little anxious, and there were whispers of a special someone meant to arrive soon.

"Who are they talking about?" asked David.

Jess shrugged her shoulders. "I presume it's a level seven practitioner, but I don't know who that might be."

David tried to catch his Aunt Gen, but just then the doorbell chimed.

Aunt Gen looked at her watch and went to answer it with a smile on her face. David and Jess followed her. She opened the door to reveal a slim, striking woman who appeared to be in her forties. She had chestnut hair, a white dress, and black shoes. She held a clutch bag under her arm. David noticed her nails were painted a blood red.

"Genevieve. It's been a long time." The woman

smiled and leaned forward, kissing Aunt Gen on both cheeks.

"How wonderful to see you, Alicia, and thank you for coming over from America. We really appreciate it. Let me introduce you to David, Jess, and the others." Aunt Gen opened the door wide and let Alicia in.

"This is my nephew David and his friend Jessica Campbell."

Alicia looked at Jess, and her eyebrows rose. "Oh, my goodness, is that little Jessica Campbell?"

Jess smiled with chagrin. "It would seem everyone knows me tonight."

Alicia walked over and gave her a tight hug. "I've known your father forever, although I haven't seen him in a while. Please send him my regards." She then took her time studying David. "Oh my, what a handsome young man you are, David Hunter."

"Thank you." David smiled. "Nice to meet you."

He knew she was just being kind, but he was instantly attracted to this striking woman. She was stunning. Her energy pulsated with a dangerous kind of power that was both alluring and exciting. Something dark stirred deep within him, and something primal awoke.

He felt Jess's eyes on him as he stared just a little too long at Alicia Collins.

Alicia reached out and gave him a warm embrace before pulling back. His entire body drank in her energy. "It's wonderful to meet you David, I'm so glad I could be a part of your ceremony."

David became aware that she still had her arms around him. There was definitely a sexual attraction to the woman, but at this range he also sensed a melancholy that emanated from her very soul.

"Thank you. I really appreciate you coming, although I don't quite know what it's all about yet." David laughed a little nervously.

"Ah! They've kept you in the dark. Always the best way with The Glowing. Then there are no preconceived notions of how it will play out."

Aunt Gen gently touched the back of Alicia's arm. "Let me introduce you to the others."

When Aunt Gen and Alicia moved to the drawing room, Jess and David looked at each other with raised eyebrows.

David looked at Alicia as she was introduced around the room. Everyone seemed really enamoured with her. Then, as if sensing his gaze, she glanced over her shoulder and caught David's eye. Her warm smile lingered a moment before her attention turned back to the surrounding guests. She clearly knew how to work a room.

His stomach flipped a little. He wasn't sure he liked the way his energy responded to hers. It was a bit wild and out of control.

"Oh Jeez, does somebody like Alicia Collins then?"

Jess asked, laughing and poking David in the ribs. "You go for older women, do you?"

David blinked, feeling a bit dazed, and shook his head slowly. "Oh, she is so dangerous."

"But very sexy, too, right?"

"Who is she, anyway?"

"I think she is the level seven everyone has been waiting on. I sense someone is a little bewitched, bothered and bewildered," Jess chided him.

"Is that another Buffy episode?" David asked, laughing as he led Jess into the drawing room.

The group reconvened after fifteen minutes, and the excitement in the room grew to a crescendo. He heard discussions of enlightenment energy, but figured he'd ask more questions later. At the moment, he was just trying to keep his nerves in check.

Rodrigo Padilla brought the room to silence again by standing slightly forward of the circle and clearing about ten feet of space. It created a break in the circle as they moved closer together. He brought David into the middle of the room.

"Thank you, once again, for your time and energy here today, and another warm welcome to David on the path of the dream dancer. Now comes The Glowing Ceremony where we find out which level David will be able to work on. As you know, the level you work on at any one time is not necessarily the level you work on later in life. You can move up levels as your energy grows and as your frequency changes." Rodrigo turned to look at David directly. "David, do you go into the Glowing ceremony as a willing participant?"

David looked around the room and at his Aunt Gen who nodded slightly. "Yes."

"And do you promise to live by the moral and ethical principles set as standard by the Federation of Dream Dancers?"

Again, David looked at his Aunt Gen for reassurance. "Yes, I do."

Rodrigo smiled and looked around at the faces in the room. "For David, this is the beginning of a new chapter in his life." He looked at David directly again. "It's probably a little more daunting given you are entering this world at a later stage than normal, and this world that you are now entering is going to seem fantastical. Whatever the age you come to be a dream dancer, there is great responsibility that comes with that title. You will be walking in the footsteps of many great dream dancers. Not only do you belong to the dream dancer community now, but you also belong to a broader group of witches and wizards." He turned his attention to the group again. "One should never forget that we are all a part of a magickal world, but we are also human beings. We have a duty to our fellow humans to live by the same moral and ethical codes by which we live our magickal life."

The room was buzzing with excitement and there was a low hum of energy flowing around the drawing room. David stood and paid attention to Rodrigo and to the faces in the crowd. He could feel the tension and the excitement. He wrung and then rubbed his hands together waiting for the next step.

Rodrigo motioned for David to take his spot in the centre of the circle.

"Thank you," David said, as he slowly walked to his spot.

"If I can ask Louisa Maycott to open the portal to level one where we have another dream dancer on the other side. The rest of us will provide the energy for the portal."

Louisa stood forward slightly and nodded at Rodrigo.

The group now focused their minds and energies towards the cleared area whilst Louisa made a circling motion with her hand in that direction. There were crackling sounds and different coloured energies made manifest, causing David to blink in wonder. The circle appeared, but on the other side of it there was someone waiting in what looked to be a forest. Everyone attending saw the other side.

David's stomach lurched a little as the excitement grew. He was actually going to travel to another part of the universe.

Jeezus!

He caught a glimpse of the dream dancer world that he was now a part of.

This defies physics. It defies everything I know.

Over the whooshing sound of the energy and the

movement of the circle, Rodrigo shouted, "David, we'll have you attempt to step through the circle to the other side. If you reach the other side okay, then please jump back again."

If! Fuckin if. What does that mean?

David looked at his Aunt Gen. She smiled and nodded her head toward the circle.

He slowly walked over, closed his eyes, and stepped through the circle. Immediately, he was catapulted through a vortex but felt more stable than he did when arriving in his lucid dreams. David stayed standing and touched the other side unharmed. He was greeted by a young woman who shook his hand and pointed toward the circle again, encouraging him to return.

David stepped back, and to his great relief, Aunt Gen's drawing room materialised around him. He was safe and sound.

The circle then disappeared and everyone in the group smiled, pleased that David was at least a level one dream dancer.

"I call on Anna Corrinn to be the circle bearer for level two," said Rodrigo.

Once again, the crackling, whooshing sounds and the bright colours cracked throughout the room.

An older woman in her sixties stepped forward, taking her place as the portal opener.

When the circle opened, David stepped onto what looked like a lake, but he presumed he would be on terra firma when he passed through.

He placed his foot on a decking-like structure in the middle of the lake. A young man greeted him, one who had obviously swum to the middle to be here. The sight was beautiful. David looked around with his mouth gaping open. The sun was brighter; the trees surrounding the lake were singing in the wind, and the water was clear and deep.

"Welcome to level two. I wish you well on your journey." He motioned back toward the circle.

David stepped through once again and arrived in the drawing room.

The energy was palpable.

The two circles of level three went the same as level one and two. Each pass through seemed to amp him up further even though he knew he should be exhausted.

There were now excited whispers around the room as David and the attendees realised he was, at the very least, a Causal, and his next step through the circle would determine if he was an Essential.

David briefly looked at the faces around him. He noticed Jessica smiling. She had her hands clasped together and tucked just under her chin as if she were praying. His Aunt Gen stood tall, trying to remain stoic, but he could see the anticipation in her eyes. Then he spotted Alicia Collins. She stared at him in a maniacal way, her smile one of extreme satisfaction.

Rodrigo called forth a young woman to open the circle for the Essential level.

David's nerves hit him hard in that moment. He felt

as if he'd pushed his luck getting this far and told himself he would settle for being a Causal.

He had asked Jess what would happen after The Glowing.

That's when the real training begins. You will need to work hard to stay in whatever level your energy is placed.

He didn't know what "real training" meant, but it had sounded ominous. He figured he would be content as a Causal and train from there.

The energy in the room crackled again as the circle to the Essential level opened.

David stole a glance at Jess to fortify himself before he stepped through the circle. A woman greeted him on the other side. She stood in a copper field lit by an orange and pink sky. A warmth radiated throughout his entire being as he lifted his right leg to step back and return to Aunt Gen's drawing room.

Just as he did, he heard a shriek from the crowd. At the moment he returned, he saw a shadow follow him, emerging from the circle and into the room. It was formless at first but quickly took shape. It stood nearly ten feet tall, definitely a male figure, with a crow's head and large black wings spanning the length of the room.

The creature looked around and finally stopped as its eyes rested on David who quickly scrambled back.

David could see nothing except the creature. As it locked eyes with his, he felt a darkness seep into his mind. Then everything went black.

CHAPTER 10

"*D*avid. David, can you hear me?" Someone gently slapped his cheek, waking him from the blackness. He moved his head slightly and tried to open his eyes.

"Okay, he's coming round, thank goodness." He heard the voice of his Aunt Gen.

David opened his eyes and immediately squinted. His head was pounding. He was offered a glass of water and gulped it all down. "Can I get another one?" he croaked out. His throat felt unusually dry.

"How are you feeling?" his Aunt Gen asked, her tone gentle.

"What happened?" He pulled himself up to rest on his elbows and then onto his hands.

Rodrigo came into view. "It was a soul searcher. It came through the portal as you passed through level four."

"What's a soul searcher?" David asked, taking another glass of water from someone.

"It's a creature that gets its energy by feeding on the energy of others and leaving them drained. Usually, they target unsuspecting dreamers or astral travellers wandering through level three without realising it."

"How did it know the circle was going to be open at that particular time?"

Rodrigo looked at the others in the room. "Bit of an opportunist, we suspect. Right time, right place. If it hadn't been for Jess acting so quickly, you might have been out for days."

David looked around the room for Jess. She wasn't there.

"I think she's calling her father just now. I'm glad you're okay. That could have been a lot more serious," Rodrigo said. He looked at Aunt Gen. "We'll give you a call, and we can arrange another ceremony."

"What? How long have I been out?" David asked.

"About ten minutes, David. You'll need to rest," Aunt Gen said.

"No! People have travelled from all over to be here. Surely, we can continue with the ceremony," he pleaded.

Rodrigo looked at Aunt Gen and around the others in concern when Alicia spoke up.

"If the boy wants to continue with this, let him do it. We shouldn't have too long to go now anyway."

David stood and tested his balance and energy.

Other than a slight headache, he felt fine. "Thank you," he said to Alicia and nodded. He looked around and noted concern and scepticism from everyone else. "Honestly, I'm fine."

Aunt Gen checked with the group to make sure they were on board to continue. All of them agreed that they would be happy to push forward. Some of the others had been a little shaken up, as it was their first time seeing one of the creatures from another level, but they seemed okay.

Jess came back to the drawing room and walked over to David. She pulled him to the side of the room. "David, you can't go on with this. There's plenty of time to do this another day. Honestly, nobody will mind. Besides, my father thinks that after being attacked the other day, this incident is too much of a coincidence. He believes someone at the ceremony may have been responsible for sending that soul searcher after you."

"Why would anybody want to sabotage this?" David screwed up his face.

"Why would anyone order you dead?" she shot back. "There's still a hell of a lot for you to learn concerning our world and the threats we face, but if you're a level three or higher, there's a lot of good you can do in the world. There is also a lot of damage you can do, too. So, there will be people who want to destroy you or recruit you."

"Jess, there's always going to be good versus evil. I might as well get this over and done with. I'll see what

level I'm at, and you can start training me like you said."
He smiled and grabbed her hand. "C'mon, I don't think
anyone will try anything now. Oh, and one other thing."

"What?" Jess said.

"Thank you for saving me, again. Rodrigo said if it
hadn't been for you it could have been a lot worse."

Jess looked at him and rolled her eyes. "C'mon then,
let's do this. See what level you're at."

Rodrigo invited everyone to gather again and form
the circle. Anyone who wanted to sit it out after the
most recent events were given the option. No one
took it.

It was explained that the circle for the fourth level
could be re-established as the mediator had been in
contact with the guard of the gate on level four and
everything was still in place.

Once again, the circle opened, and David quickly
stepped up to it so as not to lose his nerve. He raised his
right leg to step through. There was a collective intake
of breath. David stepped through and onto the other
side with no glitches this time. He was greeted by a
woman with a red hooded cape.

"Are you all right? I heard about what happened."

David smiled. "I am good, thank you, and thank you
for doing this."

"It's my pleasure. Hopefully, we'll meet again when
you do your training. Take care."

David nodded at her and stepped back through the
circle and into the drawing room. The circle then

closed. No glitches, no creatures, no harm. He caught Jess's eye, and she smiled broadly. He was now on the same level as her, which meant she could be his trainer.

Rodrigo came back to the centre and congratulated David on being an Essential. He called upon one of the older men in the group to come forward as the mediator for level five.

Sparks of energy flew towards the bottom of the circle as the elderly man opened it.

David noticed the circle for level five looked a little different. It had fewer wisps of energy around it, whereas the other circles had what appeared to be energy vines wrapped around the outer rim. This one was crisper and cleaner, whizzing round at an accelerated speed.

He and the others looked through the portal to see a man standing on a bridge, one that crossed a river of flowing water. On one side of the bridge was a sea of red roses, and on the other side flowed a sea of purple lavender. There were multiple moons in the sky and continuous shooting stars. An immediate sense of calm permeated the room. David walked toward the circle and into the portal.

The man raised his hand in greeting.

David stepped through the circle, but his body flew through the portal. His vision tunnelled as he sped forward.

Eventually, after what seemed like an eternity, he

reached the man who nodded his head and smiled. He didn't speak to David, not directly.

Welcome to the lower spiritual plane of the Superessential level.

David clearly heard a calming voice in his mind. A little confused at first, he realised it was the man speaking to him. He tried to speak through his mind, but he couldn't focus. His mind raced with errant thoughts.

What the hell?

Thank you.

This is weird.

I appreciate you.

Am I really talking or thinking?

Oh well, he'll understand.

The man quirked a brow and chuckled.

You have a lot to learn, but I'm going to enjoy meeting you in the future, David Hunter. Be safe.

David half-smiled, his thoughts still unfocused.

Thanks. In the future?

I wonder if he'll be training me.

What will Jess think about that?

What will Aunt Gen think?

Jeezus, I'm at a Superessential level!

What's next?

Oh, Upper Spiritual level.

David walked back through the circle again, but it took longer to get to the other side even though he could see everyone from the group.

A similar thing happened with the Superessential, Upper Spiritual level as he continued his progression.

The group now looked at David a little differently. Nobody, not Jess, Aunt Gen or anyone else would have guessed he'd get beyond Causal let alone Superessential Upper Spiritual. David still didn't have a clue what it all meant. He didn't know what he should do or could do, but he was enjoying the process.

Soon, it was time for the Submanifestal circle to be opened.

Rodrigo looked around the room before he began. "It's clear we are witnessing something special here today, but let's keep our feet on the ground and our hearts in the right place as we recognise the importance of David's journey and what this will mean for the Dream Dancer community." He turned and looked at Alicia. "I would now like to call on Alicia Collins as mediator for possibly the next two circles. The Submanifestal and the Manifestal circles. Alicia would you like to explain a little bit about what's going to happen here?"

Alicia walked to the centre of the circle and pulled back her long, dark hair. She quickly put it in an elastic tie as if getting ready for some strenuous work. She looked at the faces in the room and smiled.

"These portals, as we know, carry a very high energy frequency which will affect the whole group in different ways. The first circle will be opened, and when David steps through, a second circle will be opened on the Submanifestal level. Some of your powers will be elevated temporarily, and for a few of you, it will be elevated forever as you move up to possibly another level. You will be able to do more work for the good of the world, not just for yourselves. However, you will start to feel differently, see things in a different way, manifest long held desires, and be able to practise your magick at a completely different level than before. A lot of you have been to these ceremonies, although they are few and far between. All of them help elevate the group as a whole, depending on the level of the dream dancer. Tonight, we are going to benefit from David's journey, which starts right now." She took another glance around the room and turned to him. "David, are you ready?"

David felt that tingle of excitement again when he looked at her. "Yes, I am, thank you."

"Then let's begin," Alicia said as she waved her arm in the air.

The other members focused their energy at the bottom of the group circle, and Alicia focused on opening the portal circle.

The noise, at first, was deafening. The light emitting from the group built in intensity. Alicia stood in the centre of it all. She looked at David and motioned for him to step forward.

Then there was silence. The group circle still had energy flowing, the portal circle was open and alive.

David thought this had to be what it was like to stand in the eye of a tornado.

He stepped toward the circle, calm and slow. He noticed others in the group, some with their eyes closed. Many laughed at the energy flowing in the room.

It was pleasure, joy, excitement, sexual, and exuberant, but most of all, it calmed him. Almost an oxymoron, but that was how it felt to him. He bathed in the wash of emotions for a few seconds before lifting his leg to step through the circle.

Alicia held his gaze and smiled at him while she kept the circular motion of her hand going. Then she closed her eyes. He saw Jess just behind and to the left of Alicia. She, too, had her eyes closed, but they opened just in time to make eye contact. Her smile was the last thing he saw before walking through the portal.

A quick whooshing sound, and then David stood on the other side of the circle. As quickly as he had arrived, he was then transported through another circle and then a long, multi-coloured, multi-dimensional vortex. Briefly, he looked out over the world as if from space. He saw the Earth below him and the constellations around him. Suddenly, his whole body wrenched backwards, and he fell into another vortex of nothingness. He couldn't shout out, but he felt safe and tried to enjoy the experience. Then it all stopped as he started to float.

He was nowhere and everywhere. For a brief moment, his whole being had expanded into the

Universe. He wasn't just a part of it; he *was* the Universe. Then he returned to his own body, with his own thoughts. His body grew again, enveloping life itself. He expanded and contracted like this for what seemed like hours. He was the light, he was the energy, he was the love, he was the Universe.

David floated in this sea of tranquil euphoria and smiled. He floated in a world full of purple, green, blue and red nebulas. The stars surrounded him, the moons floated all around him, and distant planets could be seen for millions of years.

He closed his eyes and laughed out loud. He heard the vibration of his laughter rippling out across the great expanse.

His senses were heightened, his extra sensory perception had been switched on, and he could hear everything from everyone with no particular sounds being made. He swam for hours in this delicious feeling.

When he opened his eyes, he was back in the drawing room.

A stunned group stared at David, not quite believing what they had witnessed and felt. Some of the group were in tears, some laughing, and others were agog. David stole a look at the clock above the side table. Only two minutes had passed.

Alicia Collins spoke first. "An Elemental!"

Rodrigo stepped forward. "It would seem this cere- mony is going to be remembered for a long time to come. It turns out that David is an Elemental, a rare find in the Dream Dancer community. No doubt David's path will be a long and fruitful one for the entire community. We've already felt the awakening within us of a higher energetic force, so we have benefited from being here tonight, and in turn, we pass this energy onto other members of the community. This has a huge impact on mankind as a whole, not just for witches and dream dancers." His face beamed as he looked toward David.

Elemental, what is that?

Aunt Gen came forward. "How are you feeling?" She looked him over and took his hands.

"What's an Elemental?" David asked.

His Aunt Gen let out an exhalation and a little laugh. Other people from the group started to approach and shake his hand, even hugging him.

Aunt Gen mouthed, "We'll speak later."

Jess smiled and bowed in front of him. "Your Highness." Her laugh was joyful as she gave him a fierce hug. She whispered in his ear, "This is huge. Absolutely huge."

"Stick around after this, Jess." He waited for her to agree. She nodded as she stepped back to let others congratulate David.

He still didn't know why congratulations were in order. All he understood was the amazing feeling he had experienced, the way he had brought that feeling to everyone else. This night would tie the group together for years to come.

Alicia Collins congratulated him and handed David a card. "I am flying back to New York soon, but please call me. There is a place for you at AICILA Media in the research and development department. We could start you at two hundred thousand per year. You'd have your own driver, an apartment, and a company credit card. You'll never want for anything if you come work for me." She squeezed his hand. "I'm serious. We could work really well together."

David took note that Alicia the businesswoman was now speaking. Sultry, flirtatious Alicia was nowhere to be seen. He found that interesting.

He shook his head. "I'm kinda speechless. Thank you."

Alicia smiled and walked away. She said her farewells to Aunt Gen, Rodrigo, and a few others, and she was gone.

Something special had happened, just as Alicia said, but David didn't know quite how special.

He planned to find out.

CHAPTER 11

"Oh, my God, David, what have you just done?" Jess plopped herself into the sofa beside Aunt Gen. Aunt Gen was all smiles while Jess just shook her head in amazement.

David laughed. "Honestly, I haven't a clue as to what just happened. Could you see me in the last circle? It seemed like I was floating in space for hours."

"Yes, we could see you, and we saw the galaxy spread out before you. You were like a tiny dot. It was the most beautiful sight I have ever before witnessed. We were all exhilarated." Aunt Gen let out a laugh. "And when we got that rush of energy...well, let's just say we won't be forgetting this night in a hurry."

"It seemed as if everyone in the group achieved a higher energy vibration. It was amazing," Jess said.

The three of them sat in silence for a moment, each one pondering the experience.

"So, what the hell is an Elemental?" David said with a frown.

Jess sat back and looked at Aunt Gen to proceed with the explanations, but his aunt shook her head. "No, you go on and tell him what it's all about. I presume you will be training him?"

"Thank you, and yes. I'm happy to train David if that's what he wants," Jess said.

"Of course, I wouldn't have anybody else, except for you, Aunt Gen."

"Okay, an Elemental is simply someone who can travel all seven planes of existence and, therefore, travel freely across all the ten levels. Remember, there are two planes on level three, five, and seven."

"Okay," said David, nodding his head.

"And — this is a big, huge and — an Elemental has access to The Akashic Records. Once trained, of course."

"Great. What are The Akashic Records? We never got around to talking about that."

Aunt Gen sat forward and took over from Jess. "The Akashic Records, otherwise known as the Book of Life, are the storehouse of all information for every individual who has ever lived upon the Earth, containing every work, deed, thought, and intent that has ever taken place. However, that's our understanding of it. I believe there's only a few people who have truly experienced it."

"So, it's just a cosmic database of everyone who has

ever lived?" David asked, trying to get his head around it.

"You could say that, but it's so much more, really. It's the collective consciousness, something we tap into every day without realising. It's a record of our path in life, every thought we've had, every emotion we've felt, which can tell us where we might be heading in the future and what our purpose is in life."

"I get that, and it sounds amazing, but I don't get why it's so important."

"Without it, there is no human psyche. We forget our past, we forget the archetypes of our past, and we essentially forget evolution and everything we have learned up to this point: technology, industry, business, psychology, medical...everything we have learned is thrown out the window. We are connected to a machine that helps us function in life. If that machine is turned off, then chaos would ensue."

Jess took over. "Where do you store all your essays for Uni?"

"On my laptop," David quickly replied.

"Is it all stored on the laptop hard drive?"

"Jeez no, it's on a cloud-based service where I can get it anytime."

"Okay, what would happen if all of the cloud services in the world were turned off and all computer hard drives were erased? You would lose your essays, your coursework, all your photos you've ever taken on your phone, all your medical records, music, digital books, games, and websites. It would all be gone."

David thought more about the implications of this analogy and was getting more of an idea about the importance of the akashic records. He still didn't fully get it.

"Our very own belief systems, our understanding of how to interact with the world, how to interact with each other, would all be wiped. It would be literally every person for themselves. Chaos," said Aunt Gen, shuddering at the thought.

David considered this for a few minutes. It was a new belief for him, and one his brain, ironically, couldn't quite accept just now.

Aunt Gen and Jess let the information marinate, remaining silent.

"So, presumably, it's not like a physical library. How can it be destroyed?"

"Good question. That is for you to find out. You're an Elemental. You have access to The Akashic Records, but until you go through training on all the different levels, you won't necessarily understand any information from The Akashic Records."

David scrunched up his nose. "That's a lot to get your head around. Is this really the way things are?"

Aunt Gen smiled. "I've met with some amazing people over the years. Some have been Elementals, and yes, I know it's a lot to take in. I've experienced it many times. I just don't know how to process the information correctly as my belief filters may misinterpret the information. The high-frequency energy within you will allow you to gain understanding, and once trained, objectively interpret the information."

CHAPTER 12

*W*ithin hours of the ceremony ending, Alicia was in her private jet, heading back to New York.

"We'll be taking off in eleven minutes, Ma'am, and should arrive in New York in six hours and ten minutes. Can I get you something to eat or drink?"

Alicia looked up at the young man standing before her. "No, thank you. Once we're at cruising altitude, can you bring me some coffee and toast?"

"Of course, Ma'am." He bowed slightly and went to the back of the Embraer Legacy 600 jet to prepare a fresh pot of coffee.

Alicia slipped off her shoes and pressed the button for the leather chair to recline. She let out a sigh of comfort as she relaxed.

She thought back to the night before and the revelation of David Hunter being an Elemental, like herself.

She supposed it would take him a few years to really get a grip on astral travel and the different levels, so she had time to make her plans before he became a truly adept Elemental. Right now, he was a puppy, and he would want to play with his newfound abilities.

As she lay back, she remembered her own Glowing Ceremony.

It had been a much grander, more glamorous event. Her father owning AICILA Media Inc meant he had a mass of contacts throughout the world. They had all come to see Alicia's ceremony. She already knew she had higher energy as she had been studying obsessively ever since finding out about wicca and dream dancers. She was adept at bilocation by the time she turned twelve, and then puberty had exploded her abilities even further. At the same time, it had exploded her hunger for power and control.

After discovering she was an Elemental, she was mentored by Anya Lakatos, a Romani gypsy from Hungary. It was Anya who had taught Alicia the darker side of witchcraft. This had had a profound impact on Alicia's young mind, and she had become so used to the power and control, she couldn't understand why people would not use their gifts for their own gain.

She gathered information from AICILA Media's competition whilst practising astral travel and remote viewing. She quickly rose through the ranks and made the CFO at AICILA.

The jet had been cleared for take off, and Alicia

closed her eyes. She had completed the papers for the acquisition of Galaxy Bridge Media. She'd made an extensive list of questions to ask her lawyer when she returned to New York. Up to date and ready to take on the world again.

As she drifted off, she couldn't help thinking of David and how pure he seemed compared to her. At his age, she had been hard and determined.

He'll be easier to manipulate.

She'd already seen how easy it would be. A sexy smile, a brushing of her body against his, and he was putty.

Just like all men.

She fell into a relaxed, comfortable sleep as the jet took off.

CHAPTER 13

The journey from Glasgow Queen Street Station to Edinburgh was uneventful, but it gave David time to think about just how much he had changed over the last few weeks. He hadn't been able to put his finger on what was different now but travelling on an empty train at eleven o'clock in the morning to Edinburgh finally gave him his answer.

I have direction.

For years he had been researching and practising lucid dreaming. It had kept him up late at night. It had been his obsession and drive, the reason for all his missed lectures at university. He knew then he hadn't wanted to study law, and he had been tired of holding that truth to himself.

With the Glowing and the subsequent events thereafter, he now finally had the direction he had been missing for all this time. Now all he had to do was train his mind.

As he dozed a bit, he thought about Jess and how close they'd become over such a short time. He thought about his Aunt Gen and the newly found respect and gratitude he felt toward her.

He thought about Alicia Collins.

David had read her business card many times. He'd even researched her company, reading all about her exploits. He could still hear her whispered promise.

We could work really well together.

He still hadn't told Jess, nor his Aunt Gen, of the conversation. Everything had been too manic, and his head was still all over the place. Now that he had time to let his thoughts run wild, he allowed himself to consider the prospect of a life in New York, two hundred thousand per year with all the extra benefits Alicia had tried to lure him with. It would be doing something he really loved, something he was going to become so much better at. Looking at it like that, he couldn't see much of a downside to the offer.

David looked at the address again: Rothesay Terrace. Jess had written 'ten-minute walk from Haymarket Station.'

He texted Jess. "Just off the train. Will be there in 10. x."

"Great. I'm five minutes away. See you soon x."

He switched on the map app and started walking down Dalry Road, onto West Maitland Street, then Palmerston Place, Rothesay Place, and then Rothesay Terrace.

He spotted Jess walking towards him. She gave him a quick hug.

"Good to see you. How you feeling?" she asked.

"I'm good. Quite excited, actually." David laughed. Jess linked her arm in his and walked them to the door of what Aunt Gen had called a most prominent seer.

"This place is stunning," said David as they strolled along.

"Yeah, it's a nice part of Edinburgh. They do a lot of promotion for the West End."

"The West End?"

"Yeah, this is classed as the West End of Edinburgh. Why do you ask?" Jess asked.

"Oh nothing. It's just there seems to be something about the West End and dream dancers. You're in the West End as well, aren't you?" David asked.

"Yep, just up at Randolph Crescent, about a five-minute walk from here."

"Mm, obviously just a coincidence. So, do you know this person, the seer?"

"Don't know her well, but I've met her at Dad's house several times. She's kinda in his circle of friends," Jess said as they walked up the steps to the door.

David used the lion's head knocker and chapped it three times.

The door slowly opened to reveal a woman in her early forties...possibly late thirties, David guessed. Not what he had expected at all.

"Ah hello, Jessica, how are you doing? Lovely to see you again," the woman said, hugging Jess like a long-lost friend. She turned to David. "You must be David Hunter. I've heard a lot about you." She took his hand and shook it with a firm grip. "I'm Jean Munro. It's great to meet you."

"Thank you for having me over. I really appreciate it," David said, taking off his jacket and scarf.

"Not at all. It's my pleasure. Your ears must have been burning over the last few weeks. Your name has come up numerous times since your Glowing ceremony."

"Yeah, it's been a strange few weeks, that's for sure," David laughed. He felt immediately at ease with Jean.

"Would you like a coffee or a tea before we start?" Jean asked, leading them into the drawing room.

"Would love a coffee, black, no sugar," Jess said.

"Coffee for me, too, milk and two sugars, thanks."

"Okey dokey," said Jean as she headed to the kitchen.

David looked around the room. "This is beautiful. Aunt Gen would love this house. Actually, it's quite similar to her place."

"Yeah, I love the Victorian houses. There's lots of them over here and in Glasgow."

Jean came through with a tray of coffee and some biscuits.

"There you go," she said, smiling as she set the tray on the mahogany coffee table. "Take a seat."

"You've got a stunning place," said David, looking at the chandelier.

"Oh, thank you. I love it here. Too big for me now since my kids have moved out, but I'm loath to sell it." She laughed.

David and Jess sat on the two leather chairs facing Jean sitting on the sofa.

"Okay, so do you know what to expect, David, and why you're here?"

"Ehm, kinda." David scrunched up his face a little.

"I just told him the basics," Jess added.

"Okay, that's fine. Well, every person who goes through The Glowing, and has accepted the path of the dream dancer, will visit with a seer. More specifically, a dream dancer seer. There are many types of seers, but we specialise in the dream dancer path. You, David, have obviously accepted the path after your own ceremony, and it was amazing to hear that you are an Elemental; it's not often we find a new Elemental."

David smiled, his face reddening slightly. "I'm told that's a good thing."

"Indeed, it is." Jean's gaze held his for a few seconds. "However, although you're classed as an Elemental, you still have lots of work to do, and I believe Jessica is training you, which is great. So, my job is to look at your path and see where it leads you in the years to come." Jean smiled as she explained.

"That's the part I didn't quite get. Why do you need to do that?" David asked, sitting forward in his chair. "I mean, Jess is training me. I'm on the path of a dream dancer, so what difference will this make? Sorry, I don't mean to be rude. I'm just trying to understand better."

Jean smiled. "Not at all. I appreciate your candour. Equally, let me be a little blunt with you." She paused and smiled again. "We need to know if you are worth the investment and energy to further the cause of the dream dancers and our way of life."

"Oh!' David said, raising his eyebrows.

"You weren't expecting that, were you?" Jean laughed. "Let me show you something, David." Jean motioned for him and Jess to follow her. She walked through the hallway and upstairs to a mahogany panelled library. She located an old, black, leather-bound book and gently opened it. "Do you know what this is?"

David shook his head. "No."

Jess's eyes lit up. "It's a grimoire," she said, reaching out her hands to hold it. Jean passed it gently over to Jess who carefully flipped the pages. "This is amazing."

"It is. That book is over six hundred years old. We are trying to preserve the history of our ancestors and preserve the future of our younger generations, not just for the witches and Dream Dancers around the world, but for the whole of the human race. Our energetic signature is being depleted every year, and we need strong people to help us fight against those who are lowering the energy."

Jean carefully took the grimoire from Jess and stared at him. David looked at Jess who nodded slightly.

Bit strange.

He took the grimoire from Jean and immediately felt a surge of electricity running through his entire body. His eyes widened in shock. Images tumbled into his mind, pictures of people and places he'd never seen before. Historical places. It was like watching a period drama set in the fifteen hundreds. He closed his eyes, taking in deep breaths. The energy coursed hard through his body.

He saw himself on the battlefields of Scotland, in the villages fighting for the accused witches, standing up for them in different ways. Then he saw Jess, but she was dressed in an old brown tunic, being dragged by the hair from her home. Her children were screaming and crying. She was put on a stake to be pricked then strangled before being burned after she died. David saw himself arguing with the magistrates in court and fighting in the streets to save Jess.

The electric feeling flowing through his body became stronger as his emotions heightened.

He saw his Aunt Gen in the seventeen hundreds. His mother and father in the eighteen hundreds. The timeline moved quickly now, and he came to a group of men and women outside the temple of The Akashic Records. They were trying to destroy it and tear the building down brick by brick. David saw himself using all his powers to stop them, but nothing worked. The building was pulled down, and a huge explosion of energy shot throughout the world. Thousands of people were strewn everywhere, dying on the streets. A dense feeling of sorrow engulfed him. The darkness seeped into his mind as the energy began to dissipate. The sorrow gripped his heart, and the anger ripped through his veins.

The energy flow stopped, the images ceased, and David became aware of the room once more. Jean gently took the grimoire from his hands and placed it back on the bookshelf.

He looked at Jess with a sense of foreboding. Then he looked at Jean. She smiled gently and took his hand.

"What did you see, David?" Jean asked, touching him on the shoulder.

David relayed everything as the women listened.

He wiped the tears away with the back of his hand. "So, what was that then? Tell me it was just figurative. That was extremely intense."

Jean smiled. "That was what you came to Edinburgh to discover. What you just experienced shows you the path you will take, and if I'm being honest, it's a much bigger undertaking than even I had anticipated."

"Do you mean The Akashic Records are really at risk?" David said, sniffing.

"Yes. There are things going on just now that are much bigger than you, me, and our community, but it affects the whole world and everyone in it. What you saw was reality, or one possible version of reality, and it would seem you are going to play a major role in stopping that reality."

"What was with the history lesson? Jess was wearing ancient garments and being burned at the stake."

"Your histories are linked closely, obviously, and you've met someone from your soul tribe. Soul tribe members usually meet up in all lifetimes in different ways. You and Jess have a close connection. You share a past."

"So, we were destined to meet someday?"

"I believe so, yes. Jessica is playing an important role in what's happening as well. I don't know if she's told you anything." She looked at Jess for confirmation, but Jess just shook her head.

"Oh! Then that's for Jessica to tell you. If she wants to."

David looked at Jess and narrowed his eyes, wondering why she hadn't told him everything before now. She simply shrugged, looking a bit troubled by it all. He would ask her about it later.

"We've spoken about The Akashic Records before, but why is it so prominent?" David asked while they walked to the drawing-room again.

"The Akashic Records are the key to all of this. For centuries, men have tried to control the masses. For a thousand years, it has been relatively easy to control the minds of billions of people." She looked at David with slightly raised eyebrows.

David answered on cue. "Religion, I would imagine?"

"Exactly. And I say men because we've lived in a patriarchal world, predominantly, for the last nineteen hundred years. Still do, really, but it's starting to change. Yet only in the last fifty years. Anyway, I digress. Religion is now slipping out of popularity. Why? Because people are waking up. They are thinking for themselves. They are asking questions of religions around the world, and when you ask questions, doubt starts to creep in." Jean stood as Jess and David stayed seated in the leather chairs. "So, the popularity of religion is waning, and the people at the top of the food chain need a new way to control the minds of billions of people."

"Who's at the top of the food chain? Governments?" asked David.

Jean's eyes widened, and she tilted her head slightly. "No, not governments, but businesses, large multinational companies who want to control the minds of the masses, and all in the name of money and power."

"How do companies control the masses?" David asked. He felt like he was being lectured by a conspiracy theorist.

Jean looked at him and nodded. "I can sense your scepticism. Most of us have felt like that throughout our lives, particularly if we've come to the path at a later stage in life."

"Sorry, it all sounds a little like..." David paused.

"Conspiracy theories?" Jean asked

David pursed his lips and tilted his head slightly. "Well yeah, it does a little."

"It's okay. I get it. Trust me, David, when you've seen all that we've seen, and I mean that quite literally, then you will start to look at all these conspiracy theories in a different light. I do mean ALL," Jean said, raising her eyebrows to emphasise her words.

"JFK, Roswell, and the Illuminati are all true then?" David asked, narrowing his eyes.

Jean laughed as she looked at Jess. "Believe me, that's just the tip of the iceberg. Listen, I'm not going to try and convince you here, as you will find out for yourself in due course. Suffice it to say, there's no smoke without fire. But back to controlling the minds of billions of people. If there's a declining belief in religion, then how do you control people?"

"Media," David said, remembering the conversation with his Aunt Gen.

"Exactly. Do you know a quarter of a trillion dollars is spent on advertising in America each year? There's around twenty-three billion spent in the UK. That money is spent on trying to control you, trying to get you to buy things you don't need, or to feed your brain with information, but the biggest reason they spend billions every year is to create fear, uncertainty, and doubt in the minds of the masses. The media is creating fear and panic in the minds of seven point seven billion people. That's how you control people. Through fear!" She looked at David for a reaction.

David looked at her, trying to take it in. "It's all... I don't know, just a little bit crazy just now, all this information. So, about the fear being related to energy, I don't get that."

"So, when you create fear, uncertainty, and doubt, you lower the energy of the masses, meaning a halt in human evolution." Jean said.

"So why are The Akashic Records so important? Why are they at risk if the media is succeeding in controlling everyone?" David asked.

Jean nodded. "The destruction of The Akashic Records is a shortcut to control. If you take away the identity of the human race, the beliefs, the religion, the social constructs, and the history, then you are left with a blank slate. The world will be chaotic for a long time, but those in control of The Akashic Records will be able to effectively control the human race."

"What I saw when I held the grimoire is a fight for The Akashic Records?"

"Yes, but more importantly, you saw yourself fighting for them, even though you may not have succeeded, and that's only because you can't imagine what you don't know."

"What don't I know?" David asked, sitting forward in his seat again.

"How powerful you could be. Nobody knows that, especially you, as you're entering a new world. We already know the magick of this world, so we have an inkling of the power we have and the power we need to fight this war."

Jess looked at David as she listened to Jean speak. She then looked at Jean and nodded slightly.

Jean stopped speaking and left David alone with his thoughts. "Jess while you're here, I want to show you something." She stood up and indicated for Jess to follow her. "You're okay here for a few minutes, David?"

He nodded. "Yeah, I'll be fine."

As Jean and Jess walked away, David sat back in the chair and got comfortable.

Shit's getting real. Question is, is this the life I want from now on?

He stayed with that thought. This new world had brought Jess into his life, his Aunt Gen was a different person in his eyes now, he was starting to learn more about his mother and father, and his world had been opened to a lot of new information.

Yes. This is definitely the life I want.

He heard a whooshing noise beside him and looked around at the leather chair, "Jeezus Christ!" He jumped to his feet.

It was the little creature from his lucid dreams.

Just then, Jean and Jess returned and stopped in their tracks, staring at the creature in amusement.

David held out his hands. "Anybody?" he said, looking from the creature, to Jess, to Jean.

"He's your Watcher, David. He'll look out for you on the astral planes. He can only appear to you on the Earth plane once you have decided to truly follow the path of the dream dancer." Jean beamed at him as she spoke.

Astonished, he looked at Jess, who just shrugged her shoulders and said, "I can't tell you everything, there are some things, like having a Watcher, you have to find out for yourself."

CHAPTER 14

The drive from Boston Logan International Airport to Beach Avenue in Salem would take forty minutes.

Alicia sat in the back of the car looking over yet more legal papers for the acquisition of Galaxy Bridge Media. The sale was being held up as the Bureau of Competition at the Federal Trade Commission investigated possible unfair competition anti-trust laws. One of her astral operatives had managed to get a hold of the documents, the same one who was currently compiling a report for her.

She turned the pages of the investigative reports by Bruce Horn which outlined the reasons why the sale was being held up. She laughed at the hypocrisy of the FTCs Office of Inspector General, an independent and supposedly objective organisation within the FTC. One of their team was also in on this hold up of the sale.

Her mobile phone pinged in her bag. She fished the phone out, swiped it upwards, and logged in. A message she had been waiting on: CALL ME. It was from her astral operative.

Immediately, she dialled the number.

"Ms. Collins, I have the information you require. Do you want me to complete the report first and we can discuss it, or would you like a synopsis just now, and I'll send the report later?"

"Synopsis just now, please."

"Very well. Bruce Horn from the Bureau of Competition and Andrew Hammond from the Office of Inspector General have been taking payments from Galaxy Bridge Media to hold the sale up and leak to the press the possibility of it not going through. This was done to initiate a massive sell off of the Galaxy Bridge Media stock, which would drop the price. Then the group at Galaxy Bridge Media would swoop in and buy the stock at thirty to forty percent lower prices, at which time an announcement would be made that the FTC had found no irregularities, and the price of Galaxy Bridge Media's stock would then skyrocket again before the acquisition."

Alicia smiled as a plan began to hatch. "How many astral trips did you make to gather this information?"

"Seven trips over a period of three weeks."

"Thank you. You're quite sure about this?"

"Yes, Ms. Collins. There are others involved, but

Horn and Hammond are the two major players. I will send over the names of the others in the report."

"Do you have a date for the offloading of the stock?"

"The phased sell-off will start in four weeks."

"Excellent, thank you. I'll be in touch after I've read the report."

"Thank you, Ms. Collins. Have a good day."

Alicia ended the call and smiled to herself. She didn't quite know how she would play this, but she knew she would have to act quickly.

Alicia was meeting with her "Group of Nine" on Beach Avenue. She loved the irony of owning a beach house in Salem where she would meet with those who practised dark magick, although nowadays, dark magick was not really required due to the amount of power each of the group members possessed.

As they drove up Restaurant Row, Alicia looked out over the Salem Channel and saw the familiar sight of yachts dotted along the middle of the channel, moored up and ready for sailing. She had gone sailing with her father here many times and over to Bakers Island where they practised her mind-strengthening exercises: remote viewing, bi-location, thought bombs, dream walking, and many more powers she had discovered while she was growing up.

Over the years, she had specialised and loved her dream dancer powers. She was now adept at walking the worlds of the seven planes of existence. They used to be a haven for her, places where she would go to escape the physical restrictions of living on Earth. Since bringing the magick of the seven planes to Earth for her own gain and benefit, she hadn't returned very often. All she could ever want in the world was right here. With the help of her father, she had amassed a vast fortune, with billions of dollars tied up in real estate, businesses, gold, and cryptocurrency. She had more money in offshore accounts that guaranteed she would never have less than a billion dollars in assets at any one time in her whole life.

There was only one thing she still desired and had not been able to secure, which she could not have: power over the energy signature of the human race.

With his Elemental powers, Alicia's father had discovered that the human race was built to evolve naturally and rhythmically, and this happened when their collective energy frequency rose.

He had discovered, and at the time revealed to no one but Alicia, that the human race's collective energy signature changed every twenty-two years. He didn't know how it changed. Her father hypothesised that by opening the minds of the human race, it would speed up the process of evolution. He set up multiple colleges and universities so that everybody had access to education. He wanted to eliminate fees for education altogether so it would no longer be solely the rich who were educated. Everyone would have access to higher learning.

His numerous charities would see to it that the

highest possible education by the most brilliant minds in the world would teach throughout Asia, Africa, Europe, North America, South America, and Australia. He wanted to abolish league tables in universities and colleges and level the playing field when it came to attracting the professors and lecturers who would "open the minds of a new generation; a socioeconomically balanced generation." No longer would people clamour to get into MIT, Harvard, Edinburgh, NUS, Tsinghua, ANU, Oxford, or Yale.

Alicia thought back to her father's idealist outlook on life and wondered what would have happened had she shared the same ideology. She had shared it for the longest time in her early years, but that had all changed in one night. That night had changed her life forever and made her the woman she was today. That night was part of the reason she sat in the back of a car being driven up to Beach Avenue in Salem, making plans to halt the evolution of the human race.

She had only been nine years old when the abuse had started. One of her father's friends from the Elemental High Council had taken a shine to her. Alicia had been too young to understand, and he had threatened to kill her father if she told anyone about his physical and astral visits to her.

Alicia was quiet and didn't speak much as a child. Always had her nose in a book or three. She had retreated even more when the abuse started. Every time he would visit, she became angrier and angrier. She always begged her father to teach her the art of witchcraft.

He loved that she was such a diligent student and gave her more complex tasks and spells to perform.

By the age of eleven, she had absorbed everything there was to know about witchcraft and became adept at healing, herbology, spell craft, and her favourite: dream dancing. Her father had been worried on noticing her obsessiveness.

She had plotted in her head, hundreds of times, just how she was going to kill Anton Allard. She wanted it to be public, and she wanted everyone to see just how evil and vile he had been.

She had chosen her moment. It was at the annual Elemental gathering where practising Elementals and high priestesses, warlocks, and wizards from around the world gathered. It was a prestigious event in the witches' calendar as alliances, business contacts, business deals, and stories were swapped and shared.

Alicia had practised the spell many times, and she was ready to display it in front of the whole of the higher magickal community.

Anton had been charming as ever, and they all loved him.

Alicia had stood in the middle of the main flight of the bifurcated stairwell. Several attendees had turned around to admire her and welcome her to the gathering, but she'd had something else in mind.

With a flick of her hand, she bounced a golden ball

of energy on the head of Anton Allard and watched with satisfaction as it sank inside his head. The crowd laughed, thinking that Alicia was going to show them her party piece as a grand entrance. Anton laughed and smiled as he stood, not knowing what was about to happen.

The golden ball then re-emerged from his head and circled in the air, spreading outwards to around ten feet. Images began to appear in the circle. They had been vague at first, but Alicia closed her eyes and focused. The images became clearer and clearer, and the crowd gasped at what they saw. They witnessed two years' worth of abuse at the hands of Anton Allard on little Alicia Collins.

Anton was stunned and could not move.

Alicia's father and two other men had grabbed him, but Alicia's voice boomed and echoed throughout the main hall. "No! I want to deal with him." She quickly rooted him to the spot with a petrification spell. Then she moved closer and created an invisible forcefield around them. She wanted the crowd to see what she was doing, but she didn't want anyone to interfere. They couldn't step within five feet of her and Anton.

Alicia then raised her hands, closed her eyes, and performed a quick spell which stripped him of his clothes. She withdrew a knife from her sleeve and slowly cut off Anton Allard's penis and testicles. As she ripped the last piece of skin attached to his genitals, she performed a spell to cauterise the wounds so he wouldn't bleed out. She wanted him to live with the vile things he had done. She also wanted to humiliate him in front of his peers.

The crowd of on-lookers were helpless. They couldn't get to Alicia. What she was doing was wrong in the eyes of her community, possibly justified, but wrong, nonetheless. They had tried to get to Anton but could not, due to the powerful magick Alicia had used.

Anton had stood petrified under the spell for a full fifteen minutes before her father convinced her to break it. As soon as she did so, his screams of pain reverberated around the whole house as he fell to the floor. No one went to help him.

The display had gotten Alicia into serious trouble with the WWA, Witches and Wizards Alliance, and her father had fought hard to defend her. The board had deliberated for days about whether or not to strip Alicia of her powers with the "collaboratus" spell, which could only be cast if eleven higher witches performed it willingly together.

Eventually, given the circumstances and the seriousness of the abuse committed against her, she was admonished of the crime of harm against another witch.

After that, Alicia had kept on practising her magick, her healing, her herbology and most of all her dream dancing. One thing she abhorred from that day forward was anyone with too much power, and she had made it her goal in life to protect people from anyone with too much power.

In her mind, if she held all the power, then everyone was safe. She was doing the world a great service by halting the evolution of the human race.

She hadn't found anyone she trusted enough to love. Non-witches were too weak, and wizards and warlocks hadn't really interested her. Oh, there had been men in her life. She had needs like any woman, but there hadn't been anyone who was a true match for her. Did she really want someone who could match her in anything, let alone power?

Disturbed by that thought, she decided to doze for a bit before the group arrived.

Alicia looked out over the waters of Danvers River and watched the boats coming into the marina.

It would be around an hour before the Group of Nine arrived, so she had time to relax and think about her plan of action.

She instructed her smart device to play her baroque playlist as she sat down on her comfy chair, book in hand, tucking her heels under her thighs and leaning to the side.

She looked up from her book several times just to gaze out over the water. The magnetic pull of it had always been a part of who she was. To relax, she wanted to be near water. To play, she always wanted to be near water. To destress, she wanted to be near water. It was her energy giver.

Now, one of the most important events in her business life would play out here. With the help of the mirror, she would find out just what was going on at the FTC and whether or not the Group of Nine would have to intervene.

Her battle plan had been laid out in her mind, something that might crush the company and destroy those involved in the deceitful game they played.

She looked at the clock: 12:30. The group would arrive in thirty minutes, enough time for a quick shower and a change of clothes.

After her shower, she threw on a pair of Khaite jeans and an old grey Christopher Kane jumper which she loved and was loath to throw away.

Alicia welcomed the Group; four women, and four men. They had all been dropped off as instructed so as not to arouse suspicion with the neighbours. She didn't want nine cars lining the street.

She avoided pleasantries and jumped straight into the meeting.

"Okay, a few things we need to discuss today. First item on the agenda. It would seem we have a problem, not just with the FTC, but with the Office of Inspector General. You've all seen the report sent by the remote viewing operative. So, I am looking for suggestions on how to deal with this and also a few ideas on ways to capitalise on it." Alicia took a sip of her coffee and looked around the room.

A dark-haired woman with a European accent spoke up.

"I believe we should play them at their own game." Alicia nodded at her to continue. "Well, we have a few options. We can tank the price even further for our own gain and buy it up really cheaply before Galaxy realises what's going on. We would then hold a sizeable stake. Of course, we would have to do this using one of our outside companies to avoid a link to AICILA Media, but it's one route we could take."

Alicia smiled at that. "Yes, it's one way I had considered as well, but I fear it would trigger an alert for the SEC. Even though there would be no link back to us, they could put a halt on the sale until an investigation was complete."

The woman nodded. "Yes, that would be a problem."

Alicia looked around the room. "Anybody else got any suggestions?"

One of the men who had been very quiet since he had arrived sat forward in his seat and took a deep breath in.

"Yes, Saad?"

"Well, I think I may have found the perfect solution that could save us a very substantial amount of money, possibly going into the billions."

Alicia laughed. "I'm all ears."

"We know people in the SEC, and we know what Bruce Horn and Andrew Hammond have in mind. So, we could tip off the SEC before Horn's group prepares to sell the stock. Anonymously give them all the details of the whole group that is involved. As soon as the stock price starts to fall, the SEC will get involved. This will trigger a panic amongst the investors of Galaxy Bridge Media who will tank the price even further, but with the restrictions that the SEC put on Horn and his associates, they will not be able to buy the stock back, which would have supported it from falling further. We then pull out of the sale when the stock is at its lowest on the grounds of irregularities and the corruption that has gone on at Galaxy. This further depresses the price."

"Beautiful. Then that would mean Galaxy would come to us begging, offering up a reduced price on the sale," one of the women said, nodding her head.

"Exactly," Saad said. "I can't think of any holes in the idea, and with our connections, there would be no need to use our magick to make this happen, just good old business and a little remote viewing."

The group laughed.

"Okay, I like that. Saad, if you can make some phone calls to your SEC contacts, and if everything looks okay, go ahead and make that happen. We only have a few weeks before they start selling off the stock. The RV will continue to do some more viewing just in case the plans change. Keep us up to date with the progress."

"Of course. Consider it done," Saad said, making notes in his notepad. He stood and walked into another room of the house to get started.

Alicia clapped her hands together. "Good, that's one big thing taken care of. Let's carry on with the rest of the items on the agenda, and then we can have a spot of lunch."

The group worked their way through the list of nine items. With their growing connections and growing influence in the business world, there was little use for magick to be used to get what they wanted.

Afterwards, three waiters served lunch on the veranda. The waiters were instructed to stay inside once food and drinks had been served.

One of the women spoke up after the doors closed. "I hear we have another Elemental to add to the list." She brushed her long blonde hair back and looked at Alicia, smiling.

"You don't miss a trick, do you?" Alicia chuckled. "Yes, I was actually at his Glowing Ceremony in Glasgow, Scotland as an advanced level seven guest. Not something I expected to take part in, to be honest. I thought it was going to be another run of the mill, level one dream dancer, but it turned out to be an interesting night."

"So, did you manage to entice him over to our way of seeing things?"

There were smirks all round and even a few chuckles.

"No, not yet, but I'm working on it. He's only a potential just now, so I will let him finish his training before seeing what he can do, and then I'll push for him to join us. He's malleable, and I don't think there'll be any trouble."

"How were you invited to Glasgow? Seems a long way. I presume you knew someone?" one of the other men quipped before taking a bite of his monkfish.

"Yes, Rodrigo was Master of Ceremonies. Apparently, he knows the boy's aunt well, and he invited me to come along. However, he didn't expect I would need to do the circles for the last few levels." Alicia laughed. She stared out to the waters. "Yes, I don't think anybody expected that one," she said almost to herself.

"Should we keep an eye on him?" one of the women asked.

"Goodness no. I don't think he's a threat at all. He'll need a few years for training before he even moves up the seven planes. He's weak, still full of hormones and doubt."

The meeting continued in the same vein as the first agenda. It had proved to be very productive.

The Group of Nine was no longer just a magickal circle of people, they had almost turned into a business group. Collectively they were worth, on paper, over 100 billion dollars. Their magickal powers had just enhanced their wealth in the early days and given them advantages over their rivals. They now controlled, or had some control, over most of the major companies around the world and invested heavily in start-ups in different business areas.

After the meeting, Alicia had one last glass of wine and sat on the veranda again, watching the marina. The waxing moon combined with the lights from the boats made the water seem enchanted.

Alicia sipped her white wine and thought about David. Seeing him at The Glowing had stirred something inside her, something she hadn't felt for a very long time. Even though he was half her age, she knew there was a sexual attraction there, and she hadn't used her powers in the slightest. She knew she was an attractive, sexy woman. She didn't need anyone to tell her that. It was this thought that carried her to bed after the clock had just turned 11:00pm.

She had a restless night, thinking about business and about David. She looked at the clock beside her: 1:03am.

Alicia closed her eyes to doze off again, but David was very clear in her mind. She decided to seek out his energy signature across the astral planes, just a quick scout, and then she would go to sleep, she promised herself.

She felt his energy almost immediately, and it transported her to him. She saw him as his body rose through the dream levels to this astral plane. She summoned his astral self to her. He didn't seem sure of the astral world, appearing dazed and confused about what was happening. He would still be asleep in his bed, thinking he was dreaming, and he would never remember this.

She felt her nipples harden as she pressed up against his body and pulled his mouth to hers. It was a hard, passionate kiss, one that he had obviously been waiting on and thinking about. It was carnal and lustful...

Suddenly, a blaring noise jolted her, and she lost the projection, transporting back into her body. She opened her eyes.

Her alarm clock.

"Shit!" she shouted. She had just started to enjoy herself.

Alicia pressed her fingers hard between her legs to temporarily ease the sexual ache she had upon waking. There was no point in trying to go back now. She was awake, and it would be harder to find him.

She got up, a little angry, and took a cold shower. She didn't think about David all day as she made phone calls and conducted business from her beach house.

CHAPTER 15

*D*avid awoke thinking about Alicia Collins. He was sure he had dreamt about her and there was a definite erotic feel to the dream, although he couldn't quite remember.

In the darkness of the night, David tried again to relax his body and mind, dipping his mental hand through the floor. He imagined his limp arm, which was hanging out of the bed, elongating and reaching down through the floorboards.

He closed his eyes to drift off to sleep, all the while pushing his mental hand down through the floorboards.

Jess had spent a long time teaching him various projecting techniques, and he had been practising diligently.

"It'll come," she had told him, and his Aunt Gen had

encouraged him as well. She advised that time and patience would bring a projection about.

As he drifted off to sleep, he pulled his arm back into the bed.

Just between the unconsciousness of sleep and the consciousness of waking, David tried to turn over in bed.

He attempted to move his legs, but they wouldn't budge. Then he tried moving his arms, but nothing happened. The thudding of his heartbeat against his chest left him feeling paralyzed, as if trying to escape an unseen force. When he opened his mouth to scream for help, nothing came out, just a short grunt from the back of his throat. The darkness became more menacing, the once magical moonlight had turned evil, spilling shadowy shapes all over his room. The stillness of the night, his inability to move, his lack of voice, the moonlight, the shadows, and the dark places he could not see terrified him.

It was in that moment he realised he was experiencing sleep paralysis. The knowledge brought him relief, and he was okay with it. His fear abated as he told himself it was just a gate to go through to get to the next level.

He relaxed his whole body and calmed his breathing down.

Sinking a little deeper into unconsciousness, he felt something pop.

That was when it happened.

He could almost feel the separation occur as he floated. His consciousness was now in his etheric body. He mentally told himself to roll over and look at his form in the bed.

David's etheric self looked down, and he saw himself lying in bed.

Trying to stay calm so as not to pop back into his physical self, he moved towards the ceiling of his bedroom. He willed himself towards the window and pushed through the walls, reaching outside.

I've done it.

He floated just outside the bedroom window. Not much was happening outside, but he saw lights on in other apartments. He floated in the backyard, which was essentially a square with the apartment buildings acting as hundred-foot walls. He could still feel the wind and the cold outside.

He didn't quite know what to do next, as he'd never prepared for this moment, not fully.

He thought about Jess.

Take me to Jess.

Nothing happened. He pictured Jess in his mind, and suddenly, he was transported to a dark room. The room began to brighten, and he saw Jess lying in bed.

Oh shit, that's creepy. Take me home.

David didn't move. He mentally pictured himself back home in his bedroom, and once again, he was immediately transported to the backyard, just outside his bedroom window. He mentally breathed a sigh of relief.

As he hovered, wondering what to do, he saw what looked like black clouds floating around. They became clearer within a few moments.

Soul Searcher.

It was the one he had seen on the night of The Glowing Ceremony. David quickly willed himself through the walls of his bedroom and popped back into his sleeping body. He awoke briefly and automatically wrote something down into a notebook at the side of his bed. He knew it wouldn't be legible, but better than forgetting all about this episode.

When David awoke in the morning, he remembered he'd had his first real projection where his consciousness had gone with his astral self.

He quickly checked his watch: 7:46am

He decided to text Jess just in case she was up.

I did it. I managed to project last night. I came to see you, but it was a bit weird, so I quickly left. Lol.

David then jumped up and went into his drawer for bath towels for his shower. Bracing himself slightly, he moved into the freezing cold shower. He had started to get used to it. Jess had been right.

Once you get used to it, you won't even think about it

After his shower, he was eager to let his Aunt Gen know about it.

He checked his phone, but Jess had still not seen the message.

"Aunt Gen, I did it," he shouted as he skipped down the stairs.

"Did what?" she asked from the kitchen.

"I projected. I actually got outside my body. I can't believe it." He walked into the kitchen to see his Aunt Gen making breakfast again.

"That's brilliant. I knew you would do it. Just a little perseverance. How do you feel?"

"Oh, it feels amazing. I saw the Soul Searcher, though, and I went to visit Jess in Edinburgh, but it looked a wee bit creepy, so I quickly left." He laughed. "I didn't think I would be able to do it, which is why I thought about visiting Jess, but then when it happened, I was like, whoa..."

"Okay, you're rambling. Slow down. Here, have some tea and some toast, bacon, and eggs. Do you want some beans?"

"Sorry." He laughed, feeling exuberant. "Yeah, beans would be great. You okay?"

"I'm fine son, never better. We do need to talk about university, though."

"Oh." He grunted. He'd forgotten all about uni.

"Yes, oh! This astral world is all well and good, but it won't pay the bills."

David sat down and bit into toast. "Aunt Gen, I know you're going to be really annoyed and upset, but I'm leaving university." He waited for her reaction. She just looked at him. "I'm going to university for you and for Mum and Dad. I'm not doing it for me. I don't enjoy law.

Never have and I never will, and even if I pass the exams and get my degree, I won't follow it up and use it for anything."

"Are you sure you've thought this through?" she said in a calm manner.

"Yes, I've been feeling like this for ages, even before I learned about this magickal life. I have really thought this out until I was sure," he said, a little taken aback by her calm reaction.

"Well, it's your life, David. Do you have any idea of what you want to do?"

"I honestly don't know yet, but I've been offered a position with Alicia Collins in her company."

"Oh! Doing what?" Aunt Gen asked.

"I don't exactly know, but two hundred thousand a year, a driver, an apartment, and a company credit card sound good."

Aunt Gen looked puzzled, not to mention wary. "When did you speak to her about this?"

"At the Glowing Ceremony. She gave me her card and told me there was a job waiting for me in the R & D department if I wanted it."

"Wow! That's quite an offer." Aunt Gen hesitated for a moment before saying, "Be very careful with her. She's not the owner of a multibillion-dollar company for no reason."

"I know. I did get a strange feeling from her when I met her that night," David said.

"She's a heartbreaker, that one, and ruthless when it

comes to business. Do not get involved with her romantically or professionally. She'll chew you up and spit you out like a piece of flavourless chewing gum."

"There's an off kind of feeling I get with her, but she is very attractive."

"The devil can look very attractive, too," she said.

CHAPTER 16

The group of six men and women, including Jessica, entered the empty, windowless room and took their places on the blue rubber mats, sitting in the lotus position, ready for the task ahead of them. To outsiders, it would have looked like a group meditation session, but in reality, it was so much more.

It had only taken them around fifteen minutes to go deep into the Delta brainwave pattern and project into Upper Level One, the Etheric realm, at an agreed spot using a tree as the energy signature locator, should any of them lose each other. There were usually no problems on this level. However, it was always good to be cautious. The group called this place Dream Plane One, or DP1.

They looked around DP1, scanning for any sign of anomalous energy activity. There were none. They had synchronised their surroundings to see the same world so as not to confuse or disorient themselves. This had been the hardest part of their training on DP1. They each had a different view of the world, learned through years of conditioning in the real world, so each would naturally have a different view of DP1. They had trained for weeks to see the same world, one agreed upon in a meeting at the Institute.

The world they shared now came from a picture of rolling green hills, blue skies, and white wispy clouds. The only thing they had added was an oak tree at the top of the hill.

They looked around and oriented themselves. Flashes of light and bursts of energy could be seen and felt in the distance, but nothing unusual.

Jessica was the first to speak.

"We have a specific location to go to, and I have placed an energy signature beacon in the room where we will be meeting. Once in the room, make sure you get to the beacon to feel the energy signature so you can find it again, should we get split up. In the meantime, we will be able to get there using me as a beacon. Everybody okay with that?"

The group nodded and prepared to travel up to Level one.

Dr. Campbell looked at her and smiled. He had told her he always enjoyed coming to this plane. There was something peaceful about it, making it all the more special by having his daughter with him.

"Okay, this is where I leave you and keep an eye on

things from the Institute. Are you all sure about your roles and what you're doing?" he asked.

A few yeses and nods were his cue to leave.

At the age of thirteen, Jessica had been one of the most adept dream dancers at the Institute, under the tutelage of her father, Dr. Joseph Campbell. He had been training her since the age of eight, when she had insisted that he show her what he did at work.

Dr. Campbell had reluctantly begun to explain the world of dreams, lucid dreaming, astral projection, and the search for The Akashic Records, hoping his daughter might be put off by something as intangible as dreaming. His plan had backfired. Instead, she had become deeply interested in his research, and by the age of nine, she could have lucid dreams almost at will. Jess had even managed to astral project with verifiable results. She was what was termed a "Natural" and worked her way up to Essential then Super-essential. She was now the leader of the team.

She looked at the others. "I'll see you over there. Give me a few seconds before you follow my sig." She closed her eyes, focused on the energy signature of the beacon she'd left in the labs in a Boston Medical facility, and projected her consciousness to it.

She looked around the room, noticing the unnerving quiet. Boston was five hours behind Edinburgh time. The previous fourteen nights Jessica had travelled to this place, she had mentally noted what time everyone left, where the security guards were, where the cameras were, and the general routine of the place.

A few seconds later, she was joined by the rest of the team. They floated around the high-ceilinged office, ready to physically port.

"Are we all good? I'll port first, cover the two cameras, and make sure everything is okay. I'll give you the signal to port when I'm done."

The group nodded.

Porting was always a bit of a pain as it took a few seconds for her true physical self to replicate enough in order to transfer her consciousness into the new astral form and give it enough of a physical presence. This was the amazing thing about the astral world and something that physics would not be able to catch up on for hundreds of years.

Once she had completely ported, she picked up a piece of light cloth and floated to the cameras, covering them until they had completed their mission. She noticed that massive steel boxes had been placed on the ceilings of the room. It was strange. They hadn't been there before, but she had no time to investigate.

Jess looked up to the corner of the room and signalled for the rest of the team to port.

As she waited for them, she quickly located the cupboards that contained the bomb-making equipment.

She opened them only to find the cupboards empty. She had checked them out a few days ago and knew the equipment and materials were stored in there, but this time there was nothing. The large steel cupboards were completely empty.

She flung open the doors of the other cupboards nearby. The rest of the team arrived just as she slammed the cupboard doors.

"There's nothing here. Check all the cupboards and drawers."

They started to move when a loud screeching reverberated around the room. The large steel boxes flew open, dropping the steel shutters from the ceiling to the ground and trapping Jess and her group. A piercing noise made the whole team wince in pain as they covered their ears. The pitch became higher and higher, and soon every member of the team was on the floor, unconscious.

Dr. Campbell was in the Institute room monitoring the team members through the glass panel when he noticed the machines beeping.

Alarms rang on all the machines, indicating that something was wrong at the other end. They had all gone from Delta brainwave patterns to the Alpha brainwave patterns, meaning that their consciousness was stuck wherever they had ported.

He immediately flung open the door to the glass-panelled room and checked on his daughter.

"Jessica. Jessica, wake up." He shook her, but there was no response. "No, no, no. This shouldn't be happening. Come on, Jessica, you've done this a hundred times. Come back to your body." There was still no response. He checked on the others and found the same results. No response from any of them.

After fifteen minutes, Dr. Campbell had run out of ideas. He slowly unhooked the team members from the monitors, pulled out his phone, and made a call.

"Charles, something has happened. You'll need to come in."

After thirty minutes, Charles rushed into the room. "What the hell's going on? Are they back yet?"

Dr. Campbell's expression was grim.

"No, nothing. No response whatsoever. It's like they're in comas."

"Okay, let's get them all to the beds in the next room so they are comfortable," said Charles as he wiped his sweating forehead with the back of his sleeve. "The Institute is going to go ballistic if they find out what's happened."

"I couldn't give a shit about the Institute just now. My daughter and five other sons and daughters are in a coma right now."

"Okay, okay, let's move them."

Dr. Campbell then heard a mobile phone ringing. It was in Jessica's box. They had all placed their belongings and phones in separate boxes before entering the DPI room.

He slowly picked up the phone. The number was David's.

"Hello," Dr. Campbell said.

"Oh hello. I am looking for Jessica Campbell. Is she there?"

"David, it's her father."

"Oh, hi Dr. Campbell. Is Jessica busy? I texted her and haven't heard anything, which is unusual."

"Ehm, something is not quite right, David. I'm going to have to call you back."

At this, he clicked the button to end the call.

CHAPTER 17

"We've got them all locked in a room here at the lab. What do you want to do now?" the stocky security guard asked as he looked at the six bodies strewn around the lab floor, a steel cage locking them in.

"I'll let her know and get back to you with further instructions. Did you get the equipment moved?"

"Yes sir, it was moved a few hours before their group came here."

"Are they secure in the room just now?"

"Steel shutters are down, and energy prohibitors are turned on with frequency blocker volume turned up high."

"Okay. We're going ahead as planned in thirty-six hours, so make sure the equipment is moved to location two-one-four."

"Yes sir, it's being moved as we speak."

"Good. Hang tight and get back to me if there's any movement."

The call ended.

The man looked at the screens again through the cameras they had installed a few hours previously. He smiled to himself, not understanding the significance of what he had just done. He was just a lackey, but a very strong, fit and determined lackey.

CHAPTER 18

*D*avid looked at his phone. "That's strange," he said to his Aunt Gen.

"What is?" Aunt Gen asked as she read the newspaper.

"I just called Jess, and it was her dad who answered. He sounded really upset. He said something wasn't quite right and that he'd have to call me back."

Aunt Gen looked at him. "Hmm, that does sound a bit strange. I hope Jess is okay. I can do an energy scan if you like. I've gotten to know Jessica well over the last few weeks. I think I can get a read on her energy."

"Haven't a clue what that is, but yes, go for it."

Aunt Gen quickly dried her hands on a dish towel and walked to the drawing room with David in tow.

"Okay, I am going to go into a light meditative state, so don't be alarmed if I don't respond for a few minutes."

David watched his Aunt Gen take deep breaths in and push hard breaths out. She did this ten times and sat back in her chair, closing her eyes. Her breathing became shallow. David could only sit on the sofa and wait for something to happen.

He tried to imagine what an energy scan was and how it worked. Thinking about it made it seem obvious. It had to be like a GPS signal.

We all have a unique energy signature, and other people can find us that way.

David was satisfied with his own explanation of how it worked, but he resolved to ask his Aunt Gen to confirm.

He looked at her again, but she appeared to be having a nap. He heard her take a deep breath in as she opened her eyes.

"Anything?" he asked leaning forward.

"Nothing at all. I mean literally nothing. That's not possible. The only time that can..." She stopped herself.

"The only time you can't get a reading is when they're dead. Is that what you were going to say?" he asked in alarm.

Aunt Gen shook her head.

"I just can't find her energy signature. She may have blocked it or obscured it."

"Okay, that's it. I'm calling Doctor Campbell." He picked up the phone and called Jessica's number again. There was no answer. So, he dialled again. He did this three times.

"David, stop. There's obviously something going on."

"Okay, can I try and find her?" he said, quickly pacing around the room.

"You don't know how," she replied, shaking her head.

"Teach me. There's no point in having potential if I am not going to try and use my gifts." But he felt he wasn't getting through to her. Aunt Gen was deep in thought. "Aunt Gen. Aunt Gen?"

She turned around, snapping out of it.

"What?"

"On a scale from one to ten, how hard is energy scanning?"

She narrowed her eyes slightly and shook her head. "What are you... ehm...a two I'd say."

"Okay, teach me. I'm not sitting here helpless. If something is wrong, I want to help."

"David, now is not the time."

"Now is exactly the time, Aunt Gen." His voice rose as his frustration increased. He tried to calm down. "Let me start to fulfil that potential you've been telling me about."

"Okay, okay. Give me a minute to collect my thoughts. Go and get me a glass of water please." She rubbed her temples, appearing more upset than she wanted to in front of David.

David quickly moved to the kitchen. As he poured the water, he heard the front door bang open then shut.

"Aunt Gen, who is that at the door?" He carried the water to the drawing room. There was no reply and no Aunt Gen. "Shit!" He rushed to the front door and flung it open in time to see his aunt pulling away in her car. "Jeezus, Aunt Gen."

David closed the door and went back to the drawing room, taking a sip of the water. What the hell was he going to do now?

CHAPTER 19

*A*unt Gen drove to her friend Jonathan's like a bat out of hell. It was only a ten-minute walk to Victoria Circus, but this was urgent. She hated leaving David like that in the house.

It's for his own protection, and he would have been in the way.

She called Jonathan as she drove, and he was waiting for her at his front door as she pulled the car into the drive.

He opened the car door and led her into the house.

"Okay, what are you thinking we can do here?" he asked.

"We need to find Jessica first, and then get her back home safely."

"I thought you had tried to do that already."

"I have, which is why I called you. I thought we

could do a sniffer tracker and trace her that way," Gen said, looking at Jonathan for confirmation.

"Wow, I haven't used that for years, but it might work." He led her to the drawing room. "Okay, we need to be comfortable here. We have to relax in order for this to work. Have you used this spell before, and have you used it on the first level?"

"I've used it before but never on the first level. No matter: we can all but try."

Jonathan and Gen took ten deep breaths in and out to relax their body and mind.

Gen felt the tension in her body ease almost immediately. It was now time to do the same for her mind. More deep breaths in and out and she was ready. Jonathan squeezed her hand to indicate that he too was ready to project.

They could now see each other on the first plane.

Are you okay to go with this, Jonathan? Gen asked.

Yes. If you cast your sniffer tracker, we can get going, Jonathan quickly replied.

Gen held out her arms and opened and closed her hands over and over. The light began to seep between her fingers. She mumbled something to herself and continued to open and close her hands. Within a few seconds, there was a little ball of energy just in front of her, and it darted away quickly.

Jonathan and Gen fixed their focus on the little ball of energy as it darted through level one and the earth plane, picking up traces of Jessica. It wasn't long before the sniffer tracker stopped in Boston.

Holding hands again, Gen and Jonathan forced their energy on the sniffer tracker and were transported to Boston within milliseconds.

The sniffer tracker could only lead them to where Jessica was the last time her energy had been picked up. The more time that had passed since she was there, the fainter the energy scent grew, and her own was beginning to fade.

They floated outside what looked like a warehouse. They travelled through the walls and into the building itself. The inside belied the exterior of the building. This space was full of rooms with high-tech equipment, medical equipment, and people milling around in white lab coats.

Staying close to the ceiling of the warehouse, they went their separate ways and looked into each room.

I've found them, said Jonathan.

Gen shot to his side and looked down into the room. Six energy bodies were scattered on the ground. She couldn't make it out clearly as the energy bodies were not exact replicas and were not clothed. They looked like they had skin coloured body suits on and no hair.

Okay, let's go inside. You ready? she asked Jonathan.

Yep.

They drifted inside the room where the deafening, high-pitched noise could be heard. As soon as they got close, they had to drift back from it as the noise was obviously there to block and trap their energy.

We need to think about this, said Gen as she looked down at the six bodies.

We could create a forcefield around us and enter that way, said Jonathan.

Then we would have to lower the forcefield so we could give them energy to get out. How far could we expand a forcefield outwards? Gen asked, trying to think of a solution that would give the six bodies energy but keep them safe.

I think we could probably do around a ten-foot forcefield. I could keep the field up. Can you create an energy sphere to give them energy and hopefully get out that way?

That sounds great. Are you ready just now to cast a forcefield?

Yes, just a second. Jonathan looked to be preparing himself mentally to create one.

The air around them shimmered as Jonathan raised the forcefield surrounding them and expanded it outwards at the same time, making it drift down into the room.

It was enough to envelop everyone on the floor. Gen quickly rubbed her two hands together and shot energy darts outwards to the six people lying on the ground. The bodies stirred and looked at Gen and Jonathan. Gen then pulled her hands slightly apart and started mumbling to herself. After a few seconds, a ball of energy, that looked like a ball of fire, appeared and started to float in between Gen's hands. As she pulled her hands apart, the energy ball increased in size. The group of six reached out and touched the energy ball. One by one they disappeared back to where they had projected from.

Gen and Jonathan started to rise toward the ceiling. She closed the energy sphere down, and Jonathan pulled the field closer to their bodies as they drifted upwards.

As soon as they had cleared the room, Jonathan and Gen projected back to their bodies in the drawing room of Victoria Circus.

Gen opened her eyes and immediately collapsed to the ground, unconscious.

CHAPTER 20

*A*s David sat on the sofa and laid the glass on the table, he noticed a movement beside him. It was the Watcher.

"I wish you wouldn't sneak up on me like that."

The deep, booming voice of the Watcher echoed in this big room.

"Apologies, but I can't exactly announce my arrival. I'm here to help. I know where Jessica is."

David quickly turned around. "Where?"

"Boston. They're trapped in a steel room, and their energy is being blocked so they can't get out. They can't use their powers at all."

"What is she doing in Boston, and how can she get trapped if she's astral projecting?"

The little creature walked back and forth along the sofa, deep in thought. "There's more to Jessica than you know. We'll leave it at that for now. As for the second part of the question, she's teleporting."

"Teleporting! As in beaming yourself from one place to somewhere else?"

"Not quite. It's porting a physical version of yourself to another place, like replicating yourself at the basic level and transferring your consciousness into the ported self."

David's mouth hung open in complete and total shock. How was that even possible? He shook his head. "There's just so much I don't know." He quickly pushed the thoughts aside. "Okay, what can I do to help Jess?"

The Watcher looked at him with its small eyes. Then it reared up onto its back legs, appearing a little taller. "You can't do anything just now. I mean quite literally as you haven't a clue about anything. No offense, but you haven't. I believe I can help you in some way, and we might be able to do something."

"Okay, what's the plan?"

"Physically, I can't do anything, but I can set fire to the controls that block their energy. You can give your energy to the others in the room, enough for them to get back into their bodies."

"How can you do that? And how can I travel to them?"

The creature jumped from the sofa, tilted its head back, and breathed out hard. David looked at it and then raised his eyebrows.

"Hold on, just getting warmed up." It did the same thing again, and a flame erupted from its snout.

"Oh wow. Brilliant. Okay, what now?"

"Let's travel to Jessica. Hold onto my wings, and I'll be able to give you enough energy to project. Hopefully, quite quickly." David took hold of the small wings of the creature. They were quite strong and not as delicate as he thought they'd be.

"Now, close your eyes and get into a meditative state. As soon as your energy is ready, we'll be able to travel."

David presumed he meant he should lower his brainwave state. He closed his eyes and focused on relaxing as much as he could. After a few minutes, he opened his eyes.

"Still here," the creature said, staring at him. "I thought you were an Elemental?"

With brows furrowed, David shot back, "I've not been trained fully yet."

"Okay, okay, try again, and this time I want you to think about Jessica. I want you to imagine you're going down deep into a blue ocean. You can breathe under-water, but you're going deeper and deeper."

David closed his eyes again. He imagined he was in the ocean, diving deep and letting himself breathe underwater. Then he started to go even deeper in his mind, into the ocean. He felt the warm water all over his body and looked up to see the sunlight breaking through the waves. He slid down deeper, and the sunlight began to fade. The water became darker and darker as he slowly dropped deeper and deeper into the ocean.

He began to see half-formed shapes. Then there was a popping sound.

He was in a room with large, steel shutters on all four walls.

Where the hell are we?

He saw the Watcher sitting on one of the steel tabletops.

This is where Jessica and the others were. They're not here. We're too late.

It was the booming voice of the Watcher. He realised that communication was through telepathy.

What now? David asked.

You need to go back before you get caught. We can't do anything if they're not here, and I can't get a track on Jessica just now. Not with you borrowing my energy to project.

Okay, how do I get back? David asked

The Watcher looked at him for a few seconds. David felt stupid and angry with himself. He should have learned more by now.

Close your eyes and feel the pull of your physical body. Lower your state. You'll feel a tug or a pull, and then hold onto that pull. Get back to your physical body. I'll see you another time.

David closed his eyes as instructed and relaxed his mind. After a few seconds, he felt a little jolt and a sensation of being pulled forward. He mentally walked toward the pull and it drew on him with strength.

He opened his eyes and found himself sitting in his Aunt Gen's apartment again. The Watcher was not there, and the quiet in the house indicated his Aunt Gen wasn't there either.

Great. Now what?

CHAPTER 21

*J*essica opened her eyes and looked around the room. She was in bed in the Institute's hospital wing. She looked from side to side but couldn't see much. Moving her head slowly, she spotted her father sitting on the chair with part of his body resting on the bed beside her. He was sleeping.

"Dad." Jessica whimpered. "Dad," she said a little louder.

Joseph stirred and looked up to see his daughter.

"Jessica. Oh, my God. How are you feeling?" he said, getting to his feet. Still a little shaky, he bent over and kissed her head.

"How long have I been out?" she asked. She glanced around the room to see the rest of the team in beds. Some of them were just starting to wake up.

"It's been a good few hours. You gave me such a fright, Jessica. Can you remember what happened?"

The fog of a sore head was just beginning to creep up on her. She tried to articulate exactly what had happened. "I remember the steel shutters falling. The noise. I remember a high-pitched noise that was quite bad. I think that may have knocked us out." She tried to dig through the surface of her memories for more.

"Anything else?" Joseph asked, holding her hand now.

"Yeah. I think it was Gen who helped us out."

"Who's Gen...Genevieve, David's Aunt?"

"Yes." Jessica smiled, nodding her head and then wincing in pain. "I just remember holding onto her as she created an energy sphere." She looked around the room at the others who were all sitting up now. Some nurses were coming round to check on them.

Jessica tried to remember the fine details of what had happened when she noticed the television on the wall. The headlines caught her attention. She was about to speak again when it registered fully.

Bomb Explodes in Boston.

"Oh, my God." Jess pointed to the TV. Her father quickly turned around.

Everyone watched in silence as the BBC news reported about the eleven bomb scares and the one detonated bomb at Bunker Hill Monument.

The reporter at Bunker Hill could now be heard. "No one, I repeat, no one has been injured in this explosion, but those involved have most certainly been shaken up. The city of Boston, it would appear, is in lockdown. I will pass you over to Anna who is now outside the mayor's office building where a press conference is just about to start."

Jess and her father looked at each other.

"How did the other bombs not go off?" Jess asked. "I wonder if they managed to disarm them all."

Her father could only shake his head in disbelief. "It doesn't make sense," he said, knowing that the plan was to terrorise the city of Boston. Their enemies had been preparing for this for months. "At least no one was hurt, and we should be thankful most of the bombs didn't detonate," Joseph said, squeezing his daughter's hand a little tighter.

"Yeah, but it more than scares me to think about what they could be up to." Jessica picked up her phone.

"Oh, David called a few hundred times for you when you were away. He is persistent," Joseph laughed.

Jessica smiled as she called David back.

"Hey David, it's Jess. How are you doing?"

"Jeezus, Jess. Where have you been? I've been trying to get hold of you for ages. My Aunt Gen went away after we heard from your dad. Are you okay?"

Jess laughed. "Yes, I'm fine, thanks to your Aunt Gen, I think."

"What did she do? She's still not back yet."

"Let's meet up. Do you want to come over, and I can tell you all about it?"

"Yes, let me just find out where my Aunt Gen has got to, and I'll call you back," David said.

"Great. Speak to you soon," Jessica said, and she hit the red button. She smiled as she slid the phone onto the bedside table. As she prepared to get up, she felt a little dizzy and decided to stay in bed a bit longer.

David jumped up from the sofa as soon as he heard the loud knocking on the front door.

He opened it to see a tall, slim man on the stairs with a harried expression on his face.

"David, your Aunt Gen is in hospital. Don't worry, it's not serious. I just wanted to let you know and ask if you need a lift to the hospital as I'm heading up there." His accent had a slight German lilt to it.

David, a little taken aback, studied him. He didn't recognise him. "And you are...?"

"Ah! We didn't get a chance to speak at The Glowing Ceremony. My name is Jonathan, an old friend of your Aunt Genevieve's, but we have more pressing matters just now." He said as he held out his hand.

David took his outstretched hand slowly and shook it.

"Come in. What happened?" David said as he went to get his jacket and keys.

"I'll tell you on the way," Jonathan said.

David locked the front door of the house and followed Jonathan to his vehicle.

Once they had jumped in, Jonathan pulled onto

Highburgh Road and up towards University Avenue to get to the motorway. He looked at David and took a deep breath in. "We were trying to get to Jessica. It seems she was stuck in a facility unable to get out."

"Whereabouts? How did you find her?" David asked, bouncing his leg up and down nervously.

"Your Aunt Gen can tell you more, David."

CHAPTER 22

*A*licia paced around the room, thinking about her next move. She didn't really care about Jessica and her little team of do-gooders, although it was a bit surprising to realise Jessica seemed to be the Essential interfering with her plans. She was just a little annoyance, like a fly buzzing around a quiet room.

Still, it complicated things. She couldn't just have her killed outright now that she knew who she was dealing with. Dr. Campbell's daughter.

God, what a mess!

Alicia wasn't really concerned about Jessica right now, she was more concerned about the WWA knowing she'd had a hand in the Boston bomb scares. *What had Jessica and her team figured out? What did Genevieve Hunter now know after rescuing them?*

Killing dream dancers of such notoriety and influence would raise too much suspicion in the witch community and if caught she would surely be ostracised and stripped of her powers. Not that she cared about their laws anymore. She had all the power, money, and social standing she needed in the non-witch world to openly fight against them, but subterfuge was better.

She laughed as she took another sip of her coffee.

It's so easy. Why on earth didn't I think about that? I'll just get one of the dream walkers to find out what they know.

That was it. No need to kill anybody, just yet, and she might find out a lot more than what they knew about the Boston bomb scares.

The only thing she needed was an inside man, someone to get close to Jessica and Genevieve, to pick up their energy scent, otherwise a dream-walk session could not be performed.

She made a call to one of her team to get it sorted for her. They had contacts in every city around the world now.

Afterwards, Alicia sat back on her sofa and watched the flames from the fireplace. The sounds of crackling wood and flickering light relaxed her. She knew she would have to get back to the office, but with the lock-down in Boston, she was here for another few days at least, as planned.

I managed to sow fear throughout the whole of Boston. I wonder which city I should target next?

She smiled as she watched the wood burn.

CHAPTER 23

*J*onathan relayed the story of what had happened in the lab in Boston and how David's Aunt Gen had rescued Jessica and the others.

"So, do you think part of why my aunt is in hospital is due to her rescuing them or creating this energy sphere?" David asked, shifting in his seat to turn towards Jonathan.

"Yes, I think so. That's all it could be. It may have been too much for her. She's not used to doing this." Jonathan kept his eyes on the road as he talked.

"Have you seen this kind of thing before? Is it normal to collapse after someone has used that much energy?"

"Oh yes. Usually, it means that a week of rest is needed with lots of mineral drinks and a few magickal herbs," Jonathan laughed. "Don't worry, she'll be fine. I called an ambulance just in case."

"I wonder what the hospital can do though, if this is all related to energy."

"Well, that's what medicine really is at the micro-scopic level," Jonathan said briefly, turning his head to look at David. "If our bodies develop something sinister, like cancer, we deal with a different type of energy that is foreign to our normal homeostasis. Our cells can't fight it, and the new type of energy overtakes our bodies."

"I didn't think about it like that," said David, looking off into the distance.

"What do they do to get rid of it? They blast it with another type of energy called chemotherapy, or in combination with another type of energy called radio-therapy. It's quite fascinating when you look at how modern medicine is so closely tied to the energy systems we talk about in the dream dancer world." Jonathan spoke a little faster now.

"What do you mean when you say the energy systems of the dream dancer world?"

"Well, you know about the seven planes and the different levels we can travel to. We can't travel to the seventh plane, for example, if our energies are not in alignment with that plane. You have the inert energy to travel to all seven planes as you are an Elemental, all you need now is training. It's like you know where all the doors are to all the seven planes. You just need the key to open them. What if we could give everyone the same inert energy as you have? There would be no disease in the world."

David grimaced and shook his head a little. "What? Are you saying dream dancers don't get normal illnesses? I can't get any diseases as I have this inert energy inside of me?"

"Yes. Didn't your aunt explain this to you?" Jonathan asked.

"No." David shook his head.

"Can you think of a time when you got a cold, the flu, or were really ill?"

David thought about this and couldn't identify any particular time when he had to stay off school, or even had a cold. "What else does having this inert energy mean?"

Jonathan let out a big puff of air. "Ooft, what does it not mean? It means you will unlock powers you can't even conceive of just now. You'll be practically immortal. It also means we have a responsibility to help others who don't have this energy."

"What?' David blurted out, his mind skipping over the humanitarian part and fixating on immortality. "I'm never going to die?"

"Do you know how many Elementals there are in the world?"

"Haven't a clue," said David, still surprised.

"Forty-nine, including you. And only forty-five practising Elementals. The other four being potentials like yourself. Of course, there's probably others out there who don't even know they're witches, never mind Elementals."

"Wow! This is amazing. So, who are the other forty-eight Elementals?"

"You probably won't know most of them, to be honest, but you already know Alicia Collins and Joseph Campbell. You might have heard about others who are in the business world like Jeffrey Bezant from Cadabra?"

"I didn't even know he was a dream dancer. Are all dream dancers, witches, and wizards wealthy?"

"You'll never find one who isn't wealthy. If they're using their craft the right way, of course."

They sat in silence for the next five minutes. David thought about the information he'd just learned and hoped his aunt would recover soon.

They parked in the hospital car park and went to the visitors' area.

"I'll just go and see what ward Genevieve is in," said Jonathan.

David watched as Jonathan went to the desk and spoke to someone who pointed down the corridor.

Jonathan walked quickly through the hospital as David followed.

Soon, they were in a dimly lit part of the building and hardly any nurses were about. David guessed that it was necessary, considering what Aunt Gen happened to be. Maybe Jonathan had arranged it.

"Not far to go now," Jonathan said, his pace quickening.

They turned left and entered an even darker corridor. There was no one walking through the area.

"Finally," Jonathan said as he quickly pulled open a door and held it for David to walk through first.

Another two men waited inside the room and immediately grabbed David as he stepped in.

"You're good 'til morning," he heard one of the men say.

They yanked David forward and restrained his arms.

"What the fuck? What are you doing? Help..." As he screamed, someone punched David on his right side. He staggered as the wind was knocked out of him. His reaction made it easier for the men to drag him along as he couldn't catch a breath.

This isn't good.

They pulled him into another maze of white corridors. He looked at Jonathan who quickly glanced away, appearing a bit sheepish.

"What's this about Jonathan. I don't get it?"

"Shut up," one of the men barked at him.

After a few minutes, David was dragged into what appeared to be a dentist's treatment room. A long, flexible arm and steel trays covered in questionable equipment glinted at him. David resisted as they pushed him towards the seat where an elderly man stood with a mask and a plastic visor.

"What the fuck is going on, you bunch of pricks?" He kicked out at the tray in front of him, sending it hurtling over the masked man. The guy simply looked at him and then signalled to the man who held him.

David felt a searing pain shoot through his body as he was punched hard in the back. He fought to catch his breath when another punch came down on his face. He was helpless. There was nothing he could do against these huge men.

"Now David, we want you to play nice for us. We don't want to hurt you," the man with the visor said. "All we want is a little something that you have, something that nobody else has. It won't hurt too much and should only take a few hours. Then you can go about your merry way. What say you, mmh?" He smiled as he looked at David.

"I say fuck you, creepy little dick. This is criminal, and you'll all be arrested for what you're doing. What say you?" David pushed his head forward to get closer to the bony face of his tormentor.

Unfazed, the man continued. "Oh, come on, let's not play these little power games. A little spinal fluid is really all we need. You could be a hero to millions of people around the world. Imagine having the cure for cancer locked up inside your body, and you, handsome little David Hunter, is walking about completely unaware of his potential to do good."

The cure for cancer. This was Jonathan's plan. Hadn't he just discussed Elementals as being the only ones with the right energy to eradicate disease? They strapped him into a chair. Struggling against the restraints was useless.

"What the hell do you want with me?"

"I told you, your spinal fluid." The man made a theatrical gesture with his arms "You're an Elemental, don't you know? You're a little unicorn amongst the mere mortals of witches and practically a god in the eyes of humans." He screwed his face a little. "That is, if the human world even knew you existed. BUT...a god nonetheless."

"There are lots of Elementals in the world, and most likely better ways to go about helping people. Better ways than stealing spinal fluid. Why the hell me? I've only just found out what an Elemental is, and I don't even know how to use the powers. There's nothing I can do yet."

"Yet. That is the operative word here, David. Yet! You're what we call a potential, which means you haven't YET used any of your powers." He paced in front of David and bent down suddenly. "You're a little virgin Elemental," he said, pinching his thumb and forefinger together in front of David's face.

"All we need now is your permission." He straightened up and paced the room.

"My permission?"

The man waved his hand. "Yes, we need your permission to perform the lumbar puncture."

"Well, obviously, I'm not going to give you my

permission, so presumably you have something to dangle over me to get my permission," David said, trying to feel strong in this situation.

The man quickly turned and smiled. "Oh, aren't we a smart little cookie. Let's see..." The man bent over David, his face a few inches away. "We have your Aunt Genevieve. Dear Aunt Gen. Such a shame she gave up her whole life to look after you. Anyways, we have her. Then there's sweet little Jessica. Yes, she's in a kind of hospital as well, and the lovely nurse looking after her is waiting on a little nod from us to do some damage. How does that tickle your fancy for starters?" Still face to face with David, the man pulled out something from his pocket and stabbed it into David's leg.

David let out a loud, prolonged scream as pain shot through his left side and up the rest of his body. He briefly looked down to see a knife buried in his leg, and the man was about to drag it down from the top of his thigh.

An unexpected influx of energy rushed through him, so overwhelming in its appearance and force that it burst from beneath his skin. An explosion of anger, hatred, disgust, rage, and a carnal lust for revenge.

He watched, almost in slow motion, as this wave of energy emanated from his body and expanded outwards to fill the room. The leather straps holding him down ripped apart. David watched in awe as everyone in the room hurtled backwards, each of them hitting the wall with enough force to break bones, knocking them out instantly.

One armed guard standing in the doorway remained outside the blast radius. He raised his gun, pointing it at David. David threw out his hand and another energy wave bolted from his fingertips and nailed the guard square in the chest, flinging him across the hallway and into the wall. The guard slid to the ground unconscious.

"Jeezus, fucking Christ," David shouted as pain lanced through his cranium. Then he registered the damage to his leg and wished for a sedative. He knew he was going to have to pull the knife out.

Do it now.

He gripped the hilt, taking in a deep breath to prep himself before yanking it out.

"Aaarrrggh ya bastarrrrrdddddd."

The thought of it had actually been worse. Anticipation was a killer. He slammed his hand over his leg as blood started to seep through his jeans.

There was no way he could leave and get some real help. Not before bleeding out. He looked at his leg and held his hand over it, an idea coming to him thanks to Jonathan's revelation.

Elementals have the right energy, do they? *Heal my leg.*

Nothing happened. He noticed the bony-faced man starting to stir.

Heal my leg.

Still nothing. He thought of his Aunt Gen and Jess, and panic nearly overtook him. He had to get to them before anyone realised what he had done. He was about to give up on the healing part and simply get out of there when he noticed the shimmering energy between his hand and leg.

Heat pulsated around the wound, infusing it with a tingling sensation, and before his eyes, the laceration began to heal. The pain was no longer there, the deep cut sealed. He stood up to briefly test it and experienced no pain. He prepped himself to run as fast as he could, injury or not. Before he rushed out through the door of the room, he gave a swift kick to bony-faced man and then glared at Jonathan's unconscious form.

Traitor. There had to be some kind of punishment for those who hurt their own.

He didn't have time to process what had just happened as he bolted out of the room. He just kept running through the maze of corridors.

He didn't know where to find his Aunt Gen. He worried about Jess and wondered if she was really in some hospital with a nurse ready to inject her with something harmful.

As he ran along the corridors, dropping into one of the main halls, he felt a buzzing in his pocket.

He quickly fished his phone out.

Aunt Gen!

"David, where are you?"

"Thank God, you're okay. Where are you, Aunt Gen?"

"I'm at home. Where are you? I thought you would be waiting here to find out what had happened to Jessica."

"I'm in trouble. A guy named Jonathan came to the door saying you were in hospital, so I took a lift from him to see you. Then he had some men restrain me. Something to do with spinal fluid and saving mankind from disease. I don't know."

"That's not possible, David. Jonathan is with me right now."

David stopped short before breaking out into a run. He could hear the voice of another man speaking to her in the background. "Well, he seemed to know a lot of things about you helping Jess, or maybe he was making it up."

"Impersonations. It's completely illegal," Aunt Gen said in outrage. "Oh, my goodness, where are you now?"

"I'm at the Queen Elizabeth Hospital. Don't worry, I'm in the main area with lots of people. I'll jump into a taxi and head back home."

"I'll notify Rodrigo of this. A crime against a dream dancer is serious business and impersonating one like this is simply unacceptable. Jonathan is furious," Aunt Gen said.

"Aunt Gen, I have to tell you something else. I don't know what happened, but I can only describe it as an energy blast coming from me. I launched it at the men.

It was powerful enough to throw them against the walls of the room."

He heard a sharp intake of breath over the phone, and then the voice of another man, the real Jonathan, came over the line. "Get out of there, David, as fast as you can. Keep your phone switched on."

"Okay. Is Jess alright?"

"We've not heard anything yet. Don't worry about Jess. Your aunt and I will make certain everything is okay. Get yourself home as soon as possible."

"Okay. Tell Aunt Gen I love her."

Her voice rang out over the line. "Love you too, son." The phone went dead.

David slowed his running as he exited the building. He hailed a waiting taxi outside the main entrance of the hospital and jumped in. "Dowanside Road, please mate." He looked back at the hospital entrance as they pulled out, worried that at any moment someone would race toward the taxi and try to detain him. He didn't see anyone. David sat back and tried to relax his body and his mind.

As they drove along the M8, David replayed over and over what had happened in the room.

I actually practised magic. How did I do it?

He had uttered no command, made no special movements, and had no conscious thought to attack. He parked it on the back shelf of his mind, promising to address it later.

After ten minutes, the humming of the taxi engine

combined with David's exhaustion lulled him into a groggy state. He almost closed his eyes to drift off when the answer hit him.

Emotions. That's it. It's emotions that help bring about the magic.

Aunt Gen opened the door to the taxi and practically pulled David out. She embraced him with a fierce possessiveness.

"Don't do that again. You scared the hell out of me," she said.

David laughed. "Eh, I was trying to get to you. I thought you were in hospital."

"I know, I know. I was just really worried. Things are starting to get a little messy. It was all nice and peaceful for a while until you decided to go and be a dream dancer." They looked at each other and laughed.

Aunt Gen paid the taxi driver and followed David into the apartment.

"How is Jess?" David asked.

"She's fine. I spoke to her father, and everything is okay."

A sense of peace washed over David as soon as he entered the apartment.

Home, safe home.

And then the exhaustion hit him full force. He'd

been running on adrenaline for so long, his body needed rest.

"Go, go upstairs and have a rest. I'll check in on you later. You'll likely be needing plenty of it after this. To do what you did to those men...well...we'll discuss it later. Preferably with Jessica. I'll check on her and report these happenings to the board. We're going to need to discuss your future, not to mention your safety." She kissed him on the cheek and hurried to make her calls.

David padded his way upstairs like a zombie and collapsed onto his bed.

CHAPTER 24

*J*essica sat up and took a drink of water. She had been convalescing for four days after the attack in Boston. Her energy, along with that of the other operatives, had been severely depleted. A vitamin and mineral treatment had been put in place along with herbal remedies passed down for centuries. The concoctions were meant to restore her vital energy resources.

David tentatively opened the door to her bedroom and popped his head around. "Just me. You up for a visitor?" Jessica's face lit up with a smile, and she held out her arms.

He walked over with some flowers. He placed them on the side table and gave Jessica a tight hug. "I've missed you. How are you feeling?" he asked, loosening his grip on her.

She smiled as she fixed her hair and wrinkled her

nose. "I'm feeling much better now. I've been so tired over the last few days. They really sucked out all my energy, and I want to find out how they did it."

He tilted his head slightly. "Jess, do you think it's a good idea to go digging, especially feeling like this?"

"Now's the perfect time. I can't really do anything except obsess over what happened. Anyway, tell me about you. I heard you've had some adventures, too?"

"Nice switch," he said, smiling. His smile always tugged at her heart a bit. "Yes, I didn't just have an adventure. I discovered my magic, and...I discovered what drives it. I've been practising like crazy for the last few days."

Jessica laughed. "That's exciting. Okay, show me what you can do."

She watched as he considered her request. She had to shake away thoughts of how handsome he looked that morning.

"Okay." He took off his jacket and laid it at the bottom of the bed.

He then stepped to the side so Jessica could see him completely. She swallowed hard as the clear lines of his muscles cut through his shirt.

He cleared his throat and put his two hands together in a prayer position before pointing them toward Jessica. He then closed his eyes. After about thirty seconds, Jessica squealed in delight as David slowly disappeared from view.

She was still looking at the place he had been standing, but she had an idea that he had most likely moved. She jolted in surprise when he reappeared on the other side of the room.

She gave him a round of applause and laughed as he bowed low. "That's amazing. I can't believe you learned that in a few days. How on earth did you discover it?"

"When I got captured, something happened."

Her mood clouded over. She had been furious to discover someone had impersonated a dream dancer and attempted to steal David's spinal fluid.

And she hadn't been there to stop it or protect him.

She shook away the thoughts as David went on to relay the events at the hospital. Jessica was genuinely excited that his magickal powers had naturally manifested when he needed them most, although, it would have been even better had the circumstances not been so dire.

"You probably know this already, but I had a bit of a revelation about magic. It's all to do with emotion. I figured I couldn't have done what I did at the hospital without feeling a particular emotion," David said, getting caught up in the excitement of sharing this with her.

"Yes, we're taught that from an early age, but for me it didn't really sink in until I was older. This is amazing, David. Connecting to your emotions will really speed up your training." Jess looked out the window as her words trailed off.

"What is it?" he asked.

Jess took a deep breath. "You know you'll probably get recruited, right?"

"Recruited for what?"

"Your skills will be highly sought after by lots of different types of organisations. And, I hate to say it but there's several of them, and they'll all want to either hire you, kill you, or just keep an eye on you."

"Whoa, that's pretty depressing," David said, coming to sit next to her on the bed.

She placed her hand on his arm to comfort him. "I know, and I'm sorry, but it's the truth. There have been a lot of unexplained deaths within the dream dancer community. Think about the power they have and think about what you could do with that power."

She studied David as he looked out the window and mulled over her words. The sun peeked its way through the buildings opposite to rest on the park.

"What do I do then? I mean, I haven't a clue about all of this, but in the space of a week, I was attacked, you were captured, your energy sucked dry, my Aunt Gen put herself in danger, and then a deranged doctor went after my spinal fluid. Is this the life of a dream dancer?"

Jess could only look at him and purse her lips. She knew that for herself and David it would be.

There was a silence that marinated for a few minutes. "Up until now, my life has been pretty simple," David said. "And pretty unexceptional. Routine, really. Get up, study, make a living, go out drinking with friends, pass a few exams. It's not the future I want for myself."

Jess held her breath and waited for him to continue, hoping he would say what she wanted and needed, what they all needed.

"I don't think practising law, getting married, and having that whole white-picket-fence lifestyle is my path, Jess."

She smiled as he seemed to shudder at the thought.

"I agree. I think you're meant for much more."

David smiled and grabbed her hand. "However, this life seems like a short one. Practise magick, dream dancing, lose loved ones, get killed in the process."

"Or," Jess said softly, "we train you to be exactly what this world needs. Surely you've always wanted to be a superhero," she teased.

"So, I perfect the art of magick, perfect the art of dream dancing, save a bunch of people from getting killed, stop the bad guys from doing harm to others, and live a fucking exciting life."

David smiled and turned to Jess. "And I get the girl."

Jess let out a big belly laugh. "Let me know when you find her. I'll have to approve, first." David gave her a meaningful look that she was too nervous to acknowledge. "So, what have you decided?"

"It seems I can do more good by really learning the craft of magick and dream dancing, which is strange as I hate studying." David laughed.

Jess didn't laugh. She looked down at her bedsheets

and back to him. "David, this is not a great life to have. It might sound exciting. It's a bit like most young men wanting to fight in a war. The initial concept sounds so exciting and adventurous, but the realities of war soon hit home. I want to be perfectly upfront about that."

"I know. But isn't life a big risk anyway? I mean, I could cross the road and get hit by a bus tomorrow." David laughed, but Jess wasn't playing.

"The difference is you're not waiting for the buses to come along only to jump out in front of them. That's essentially what you're doing if you decide to truly live this life and work with the DDA."

"The DDA?"

"Sorry, the Dream Dancers Assembly. We've never really spoken about it before. God there's so much to tell you, but you really need to be sure about what you're doing here, David. You're already viewed as a threat to some and invaluable to others."

"Jess, my life path just now is leading nowhere. I've been studying law for two years, and I don't even like it. I get through the monotony by drinking with my mates and just partying as much as I can, but I've been studying lucid dreaming for years of my own volition and it's something I love. It turns out I can take what I love ten steps further by learning magick, and dream dancing, AND my family already does it, AND I just met an amazing friend who can show me the ropes."

"Ah, thank you!' Jess smiled and tilted her head to the side.

"Oh, I wasn't talking about you. I was..."

She launched a pillow, hitting David square in the face as they both laughed.

"So, you've made up your mind then?" Jess asked, looking serious again.

David looked at her, making her insides melt as his warm smile spread across his face. "I've found my purpose, Jess. I just need someone bossy and over-bearing who's willing to teach me," he said, raising his eyebrows teasingly.

Jess pointed to herself and laughed. "Moi? Bossy and overbearing? Hand me that pillow."

David grabbed her wrists and chuckled as she went for her weapon. The touch of his skin heated her core. Their gazes held and his eyes softened.

He might very well be the death of her, but what a way to go.

"It would be a pleasure, David Hunter. I think we're gonna have some good adventures together."

The End
(Actually, it's just the beginning!)

CAN YOU DO ME A FAVOUR

*R*eviews are the most powerful tools in my little toolbox when it comes to getting attention for my books. As much as I'd like to have, I don't have the finances like the big publishers do to market my books.

However, I do have something much more powerful than money and **that is you**. If you liked the book please leave an honest review of the book on amazon and tell a few of your friends about it on social media.

You can leave a review by clicking the link below

. . .

Review The Dream Dancers Book 1

Thank you so much in advance.

If you liked this book you can check out the rest of the books in the series: https://geni.us/WoSSeries

ACKNOWLEDGMENTS

The Witches of Scotland community on Facebook are the most amazing bunch of people and I couldn't have completed this without them.

I would also like to thank you, the reader. I hope you enjoyed the first book in this serial, enough to make you want to read the 2nd one.

I also want to thank the beta readers and the ARC readers who gave me invaluable support whilst writing this. Special thanks goes to Kim, who found a ton of grammatical errors, so much so that I hired her as a proof reader.

Also a huge thank you to C J Anaya, my book coach, developmental editor, and line editor and an amazing writer in her own right. Her videos on writing a series are great and gave me the confidence to start writing this series.

Most of all I would like to thank my wife, Sharon, for being my first reader and telling me that the story 'is really good.' and generally for all her support with all my crazy solo careers, hopefully this is the last one babe.

ABOUT STEVEN AITCHISON

Steven is just an ordinary guy who likes to make up stories for a living.

He lives in the West End of Glasgow, yes in the Golden Triangle. When he is not writing he loves spending most of his time with his wife, his two grown sons and his family.

If you would like to find out more about Steven follow him online

Email:
authorsteven@stevenaitchison.co.uk
TikTok Page:
www.TikTok.com/@steven_p_aitchison
Facebook Author Page:
www.facebook.com/StevenAitchisonAuthor

Facebook main page:
www.Facebook.com/ChangeYourThoughtsToday
Instagram:
www.instagram.com/StevenPAitchison
Youtube:
www.Youtube.com/StevenAitchisonCYT

Made in the USA
Monee, IL
03 January 2025

126f72ee-54b5-48cc-bc3d-d802c4d7d5dbR01